Mistletoe Mischief

A SHADOW OPS TEAM NOVELLA

Makenna Jameison

ISBN: 9798870409870

ALSO BY MAKENNA JAMEISON

SHADOW OPS TEAM

Jett
Ford
Luke
Sam

Table of Contents

Chapter 1

Shadow Ops Team leader Jett Hutchinson strode across the parking lot of Shadow Security, the chilly winter air biting into him. His early meeting in the city had gone well, but he was eager to get back to the office and see his fiancée. It was hard to believe it had been more than a year since he'd first met Anna Dubois at a swanky bar in Manhattan. He'd bought her drinks and dinner and then taken her back to his place in upstate New York for the weekend. She'd come home with him the night they met and essentially never left. After a whirlwind courtship, he'd proposed. Now they had a new baby and a wedding to plan, plus she was pregnant. Again. Jett never had been able to keep his hands off his tempting better half, and Anna always loved to tease and entice him.

He smiled, shaking his head.

Life was damn perfect.

"Good morning," his receptionist Clara said as he swiped his badge and moved into the lobby, the cold air disappearing behind him as the heavy doors swung shut. There was a big wreath hanging on the wall behind the receptionist's desk, and there was a large Christmas tree with white lights in the corner. Anna's doing. He'd never seen much reason to decorate the office in prior years.

"Good morning, Clara," Jett said smoothly, striding over to the front desk.

"How'd the meeting go?" she asked.

"Fast-paced and furious, just like always. The Feds keep us on our toes. We've got multiple things coming down the pipeline, but I trust you and Anna will be able to keep us organized."

"It's nice to have her back," Clara said.

Jett's lips quirked. "I tried to convince Anna to continue her maternity leave indefinitely, but you know my fiancée—strong-willed like me," he said with a low chuckle. "Our compromise was that she works part-time for now."

"I think she misses your little guy more than she wants to admit when she's here," Clara said. "Brody is adorable. I heard her trying to convince the nanny to bring him for a visit to headquarters the other day," she confessed. "It must be hard to leave him."

"I suspected as much. You know Anna, though. She always wants to do things her way. Since you're manning the phones for Shadow Security and keeping everything up here organized, I'll probably have to look into getting more administrative help on the Shadow Ops Team side. How was your weekend?" he asked, changing subjects.

"Good," Clara said. "We picked out a Christmas

tree—a real one this year. The pine needles are driving me crazy, but Eloise loves it. She has Ford wrapped around her finger. She's convinced him to put lights up on the roof so Santa and his reindeer can find us." Clara shook her head, smiling. "Eloise is going to have us busy nonstop getting ready for Christmas."

"I kept the boss busy this weekend," Anna teased as she walked in, winking at the quiet receptionist, who immediately looked flustered. Anna's blonde hair swished around her, and her blue eyes twinkled in amusement.

Jett squeezed Anna's waist in warning as he pulled her close, loving the way her slender arms wrapped around his neck and full breasts pressed against his chest. Her sweet scent surrounded him as he murmured hello. Anna was anything but shy—outspoken, impulsive, and headstrong were more accurate descriptions. She was a handful, and he was crazy in love with her. It was somewhat surprising given that Jett was a man who hadn't previously believed much in relationships. He was busy running his own security company and didn't have time for frivolous things or clingy women. Anna was as independent as they come, a perfect match for him. She'd shaken his world around like one of those snow globes that were so popular around the holidays. He didn't know which way was up sometimes with Anna, but he wouldn't change a second of it.

He kissed her gently, loving the feel of his lips pressed against hers, then extricated himself from her arms, clasping her hand instead. "Don't mind Anna," he said dryly.

"No one minds me," Anna assured him. "I bring

some much-needed life to the office," she added with a wink.

"Well, there's certainly never a dull moment with you around," Clara said generously.

The doors to the basement opened before Jett could respond, and several members of the Shadow Ops Team strode in. "Boss, you're back," Luke Willard said as he came over. "We were downstairs doing some shooting at the range. How'd the meetings go?"

"Good," Jett replied, watching as Sam Jackson and Gray Pierce walked over to join them. Aside from a gun range, the large headquarters complex had a full gym and armory, not to mention countless offices and conference rooms equipped with the latest IT and communications equipment. It was perfect for the men to train and be readily available for briefings, taking on new missions as they arose. "We'll be meeting soon. There are several new things my contact at DOD had for us, one more pressing than the others."

"Anything big?" Gray asked.

Jett's eyes landed on him, and he subtly nodded. The men couldn't discuss classified details in the lobby. Even though Jett trusted Anna and Clara, it was safer for them both if they didn't know the specifics of any given operation. Besides, they didn't have the clearances he and his men did. All their meetings were held behind closed doors in the secure section of the building. Nothing was left to chance, and they operated much as any of the government agencies did, although on his terms. Jett had left the military behind years ago, choosing how and when they operated.

"There's always someone out there causing problems," Luke said with a frown. "Can't the bad guys stop working in December like the government?"

Jett barked out a laugh. "Those Feds don't get much done at the end of the year, do they? Gotta burn through all the annual leave they accrue. We all know the military doesn't operate that way, however. There are boots on the ground all over the world and countless situations being monitored."

"Who's causing problems this time?" Ford asked as he walked in carrying two large boxes of donuts, the chill of the winter air briefly whipping through the lobby. Jett raised his eyebrows. "I ran out to grab donuts on my lunch break," Ford said with a flash of amusement in his eyes. He set them down on the front counter, glancing over at his wife, Clara. "The two pregnant ladies were craving something sweet."

"You're too good to us," Anna said with a wink, pulling Jett with her over to the boxes as the others watched in amusement. "Thanks for running out to get them."

"How are you feeling?" Ford asked.

Anna brushed a strand of her blonde hair back, beaming. "Much better now that my morning sickness has subsided. Let's just hope it stays away for the rest of the pregnancy. I'm jealous of Clara," she joked.

Clara's gaze flicked toward them. "Somehow, I lucked out with having fairly easy pregnancies. I'm thankful, since Eloise is basically a nonstop ball of energy. You'd think kindergarten would tire her out, but I guess that was wishful thinking on my part."

"I'll take her to the indoor playground tonight,"

Ford promised. "It gets dark so early, we can't do much outside. That should tire her out some— maybe. The kid does have endless energy."

"Aw, you're the best bonus dad," Anna said.

Jett watched as his fiancée snagged a pink frosted donut, taking a dainty bite. Her bracelets jangled with the movement, and his gaze caught on her pretty lips. She had on the pink lipstick he loved, and the hot pink nail polish on her fingertips was feminine and sexy. Although Jett was a gruff, no-nonsense man, he appreciated how Anna enjoyed putting effort into her appearance. While he didn't understand all the hair, nails, and God knows what other appointments she scheduled, he appreciated the results. She was stunning.

Anna's necklaces dangled between her breasts as she turned back toward him, and he'd noticed recently how they were even fuller now that she was pregnant again. Anna was barely showing yet, the tiny swell of her stomach the only thing giving away baby number two. Even that was for his eyes only, because you couldn't detect it yet in the slim pants and cashmere sweater she wore. He enjoyed undressing her slowly each night and lavishing her with attention, his hands and mouth everywhere. Jett had learned early on that she was only too happy to be the object of his affections.

"You should try a donut, baby," she said, taking another bite. Jett's gaze moved from her pink lips to her eyes, seeing the amusement in them. Anna knew he could never resist her.

"Maybe later," he murmured, his hand briefly running over her long, blonde hair. Anna was sexy and drop-dead gorgeous, but she made him laugh and feel lighter than he ever had during his military career and subsequent career at Shadow Security. The black ops team he ran was kept under wraps, but she knew the gist of what went on. He'd never involve her in the dangerous parts of their missions, but having her support was something he'd never take for granted. She was so organized and efficient at running things in an office, he'd even hired her at his company when she quit her high-stress job on Wall Street.

"These donuts are good," Sam said, finishing off his. "Thanks for thinking of us, buddy," he joked to Ford.

Ford was talking quietly with Clara but chuckled, nodding at his teammate. "Gotta keep the missus happy," he joked.

"Pregnancy cravings are so weird," Clara said. "I didn't want anything sweet when I was pregnant with Eloise, but now it's like I just can't get enough."

"Well, I for one appreciate them very much," Sam said with a wink. "Next time I don't feel like grabbing lunch, I'll just get you ladies to send Ford out again. Let me know if you need ideas on what he should grab for us, all right?"

"Not a chance," Ford muttered as the others laughed.

The rest of the men were polishing off their own donuts, and Jett nodded to the door. "Let's move to the conference room for our briefing. I've got multiple updates to share, and time is pressing on one. We need to make haste."

He turned toward Anna, leaning down as his hand landed at her waist. "I'll see you tonight, sweetness." His thumb rubbed against the soft cashmere, and Jett didn't miss the way she shivered slightly at his touch.

She rose up to her tiptoes and gave him a quick kiss. "I'm heading home to baby soon. You know your son was up screaming all night," she added unnecessarily.

"He's a night owl like his parents," Jett quipped. "And how could I forget? I had big plans for us last night that would've worked better with a sleeping baby."

"I asked the nanny to stay tonight," she said with a sly smile. "Hope that's not a problem. I could use some uninterrupted…sleep."

Heat rose within him as she pressed even closer. "Sounds perfect," he said, his voice husky. He kissed her once more but then turned, heading toward the doors leading to the secure section of the building. As much as he'd love to remain right here with his fiancée, or better yet, take her home and straight to bed, the team had work to do.

***

"He works too hard," Anna said as the rest of the men filed out. The lobby felt quieter without all the masculine energy in the space. Sometimes that group of alpha males felt like it sucked up all the air in the room. They were all intense and protective, used to being in charge, and Anna loved when Jett turned all that gruff masculinity on her.

She moved behind the desk, grabbing the stack of folders she'd set there earlier.

"I guess you have to work hard if you run your own company," Clara pointed out. "He's not exactly the hands-off type."

"For real. I mean, he can never keep his hands off

of me," Anna joked. Her gaze flicked over, and she saw the quiet receptionist blushing. "Oh, come on. I know Ford is the same way with you. The man is smitten. He rushed out just to get donuts for you on his lunch break."

Clara smiled. "That was sweet. He's really overprotective now with my being pregnant. I swear he doesn't want me to lift a finger at home. I had to remind him that I was alone and pregnant with Eloise when her father was pretty much absent. Of course, that just makes Ford all the angrier. He likes to take care of people."

"Especially his wife," Anna teased. "Mr. and Mrs. Ford Anderson does have a nice ring to it. Speaking of rings, Jett and I have been engaged for a year. I told him I wanted to wait until I had the baby before planning our wedding, and then bam! Pregnant again."

"That must have been such a total shock for you."

"A shock, yes, but we're over-the-moon excited." Anna set the stack of folders back down, moving closer to Clara. "I mean, we weren't preventing it exactly, I just didn't think it would happen that soon. I always wanted a houseful of kids, so it'll just happen sooner rather than later. I had the best idea the other night though. Jett thinks I want to wait another entire year for our wedding now that I'm pregnant again. I mean, that's what I said all along, right? No wedding dress with a baby bump." Her hands ran over her flat stomach. There was the barest hint of a swell, but Anna knew only she and Jett noticed it. "I'm feeling pretty good now with the morning sickness gone. I want to surprise Jett with a wedding."

"What?"

"Yep," Anna said with a grin. "He's always doing things for me—buying me gifts, bringing home flowers. How shocked would Jett be if he showed up in our backyard to his own wedding?"

"Wait—he'll come not knowing he's the groom?"

"Yes," Anna insisted, laughing. "I'll get the guys to distract him with something important or tell him we have plans that night. He'll be in a suit, I'll be in a wedding dress, and we'll get married right there in front of all our family and friends. I'll plan everything so he doesn't need to worry about it. Seriously, the man is stressed out enough half the time running all their missions. I know he wants to make it official, especially now that we have a child. Why wait any longer to marry the man I love?"

Clara smiled, tears forming in her eyes. "Shoot. I forgot about these darn pregnancy hormones." She shook her head, trying to get control of her emotions. "If anyone could pull it off, it would be you. But when would you have the wedding?"

"Before Christmas," Anna said.

"That's only a few weeks away," Clara said in disbelief.

"It is, which means I'll have my work cut out for me. It'll be worth it to see the expression on his face. I'll go dress shopping, buy some sexy lingerie for my wedding night. Shoot, maybe Lena can book the honeymoon for me," she said, referring to Jett's assistant. "But I'll plan the food, music, bartender— everything. I know it's last-minute notice, but hopefully most people can come. When I send out invitations, I'll tell everyone to text me their response. He'd notice if I suddenly got a slew of RSVPs in the mail."

"Only you, Anna," Clara said. "I suspect he'll know you're up to something anyway."

Anna lifted a shoulder, smiling. "Yes and no. While he may realize something is going on, Jett will just assume it's a Christmas gift. I did decorate for the holidays," she said, glancing across the lobby. "A surprise wedding isn't even a possibility in his mind."

"Well, you got me there. I figured you'd book some fancy place in Manhattan and pull out all the stops, maybe go dress shopping at one of those boutiques you always see on TV."

"The TV shows where the bride chooses her dress?" Anna asked with a laugh. "That would be fun. We'll keep the ceremony and reception relatively small—family, close friends. I need to call his brother."

"Slate?" Clara asked, referring to Slate Hutchinson, the commander of several Navy SEAL teams in Coronado.

"Yep. We've only met twice. He was less than impressed that we got engaged so quickly last year," Anna recalled with a giggle. "He got over it once he met me. We hoped to get out there and visit over the past year or head to Jett's cabin in the mountains, but I was sick throughout the pregnancy, and now we've got a baby." Anna lifted a shoulder. "It's not exactly an ideal time for a cross-country flight. I know Slate's got a hectic schedule like Jett what with saving the world, but hopefully he'll be able to come on short notice. I think he's got tons of leave saved up since he never takes a vacation. Oh, I need to call Ashleigh and Jen. I would say that they'd be shocked about my last-minute surprise wedding but they know me too well."

"Only you, Anna."

"You just said that."

"Well, it bears repeating," Clara teased, but Anna could see the smile she was trying to hide.

"I'm going to do it—just pick a date and shock the hell out of him. Married before Christmas," she said with a smile. "Baby Brody won't even remember his first Christmas this year, so next year we'll be doing it up big. Plus, we'll have another baby by then."

"I think it's perfect," Clara said. "If anyone can pull it off, it's you. Let me know if you need help."

"Absolutely. You did just get married yourself. I've got to finish up with these files," Anna said, glancing at the folders she'd set back down. "But once I get home, I'm going into wedding planning mode. I'll text you later with the date. This is going to be a full-blown secret mission," she said, her gaze landing on the mistletoe that she'd hung none-too-discreetly in the middle of the doorway. "Operation Mistletoe Mischief is underway," she said with a wink, grabbing her badge and moving across the lobby as Clara called out goodbye. Anna swiped her badge at the secure doors and walked down the hall, smiling. She needed to finish up with inventory and some paperwork so she could start wedding planning and shock the hell out of Jett.

Chapter 2

Jett muttered a curse as he climbed out of his vehicle, shutting the door. He'd stayed hours longer than he intended but had needed to brief the team on several unfolding situations. He was late for dinner, which was par for the course much of the time, but fortunately, Anna always understood. She'd worked ridiculous hours on Wall Street before they'd met and knew he had a fast-paced career running his own security firm and black ops team. Still, he was eager to see her even though only mere hours had passed.

His gaze tracked to the nanny's car in the driveway as the garage door shut, and his lips quirked. A night alone with sweet Anna was exactly what he needed after his stressful day. While they both loved their little guy beyond words, life with a newborn baby left them with little uninterrupted alone time. It was hard to believe that next Christmas they'd have not one, but two kids. He shook his head. Him—a family man.

Wonders never ceased.

Jett punched in the alarm code and opened the door to his large home quietly. Although the baby was probably down for the night, with the nanny handling the late feedings to give Anna a much-needed reprieve, he didn't want to risk waking Brody up. Jett strode through the foyer and smiled as he saw Anna moving around the kitchen, her blonde hair shimmering down her back in the warm light. She'd changed into a camisole and leggings and while nothing about it was overtly sexy, she was still utterly breathtaking.

Anna turned at that moment and squealed in delight, rushing over to him. Jett caught her in his arms, laughing. "You seem excited," he said after giving her a heated kiss and setting her back on her feet.

"Just happy you're here is all," she said, smiling up at him.

"You're up to something," he murmured. He stepped closer, inhaling her peaches and cream scent as he brushed some of her hair back.

"Me?" she asked, her blue eyes twinkling. He didn't miss the catch of her breath as his thumb trailed over her skin. "If I was, it might be your Christmas present, so you can't ruin the surprise and ask questions."

"Um-hmm," he murmured, ducking lower as he nuzzled against her neck, the scruff of his jaw causing her to shiver. His lips brushed against her soft skin. It never failed to amuse him that she smelled sweet all over. Positively edible. He kissed her neck again, letting his lips linger. There was nothing more that he wanted than to simply devour her. "What are you hiding, sweetness?"

His hand on her hip trailed lower, and then he was palming her firm, round bottom as he pulled her even closer. Jett's erection pressed against her stomach, and Anna playfully teased him. "Down boy." He nipped at her neck, squeezing one cheek of her bottom through the leggings.

"He's just eager to get inside you," Jett said, his voice gravel. "Are we alone?"

"Completely. The nanny is in the other wing with baby Brody, and he's down for the night. Why?" she asked, feigning innocence.

"I need you." His voice was deep. Strained. His cock was pressing against the confines of his boxer briefs, swelling even more at the thought of stripping Anna bare right here in his kitchen. Their kitchen. His home had been big and empty before she'd moved in, and now it was filled with laughter and love. Now they were a family.

Anna pulled back, her breasts rising and falling against the tight camisole, so ripe and tempting. Her nipples pebbled against the soft fabric. "Then take me," she said, reaching down to pull her top off. Her breasts bounced free, and his cock twitched. She tossed her camisole onto the counter, her long, blonde hair falling around the full globes of her breasts, teasing her nipples. He stilled, taking in the sight of the goddess before him. Anna nude was a sight to behold, nothing but soft skin and tempting curves.

"So pretty," he said, backing her against the counter. His hands were on her breasts, teasing, his thumbs rubbing her taut buds as she moaned. "You're even more sensitive now." He ducked, sucking one pink bud into his mouth as Anna squirmed. He pulled away for a moment, lifting her onto the counter, and then he was sucking and laving at her nipples again, teasing her. Anna's hands landed on his head, her fingernails scratching through his short-cropped hair.

"Mine," he ground out, feasting on her sensitive breasts. He nipped and sucked until he could see she was already close, gasping as he held her in place on the countertop. Jett's erection was thick and throbbing, but he needed to make her come undone first. His hand slid up her slender thigh until he reached her core, his thumb toying with her sex through the thin material of her leggings. Anna gasped as he found her clit, and Jett smiled against the creamy skin of one breast. "You're wet," he said, rubbing her swollen bud in tiny circles.

"Oh God," she panted, frantically clinging to him as her hips moved of their own volition.

"And you're wearing too many clothes." Jett eased her back on the hard counter, wishing he'd thought to throw down a towel so she wouldn't be uncomfortable. "I should get a blanket for you," he said, pausing.

"No. Hurry!" Anna was already gasping and pleading with him, and he tugged her leggings down, enjoying the sight of her bare pussy. The leggings fell to the floor, forgotten. His big hands slid back up her legs, touching the sensitive skin behind her knees as she shivered. He held her legs spread apart for a moment, enjoying the sight of his woman lying before him. She was glistening with arousal, wet and ripe for him. He grasped her legs more tightly as he moved closer, lifting them over his shoulders. His hands curved around her waist, his mouth hovering over her pussy, but he moved higher, kissing her stomach. His child was growing inside her, and she was his in every way.

"Sweet Anna," he said as he kissed his way lower, nuzzling the scruff of his jaw against her bare sex. Jett's thumbs spread her pussy lips, and then Jett was feasting on her, listening to her tiny mewls and whimpers. She was even sweeter now that she was pregnant again, and he licked and laved at her, savoring her taste. His cock was throbbing, rock hard, and he sucked her clit into his mouth, lightly biting down as Anna tried to conceal her cries.

He pressed closer, her legs spread helplessly wide over his shoulders, and then he devoured her, not letting up until she was screaming his name. Anna was still gasping as he shifted her legs down and pulled his erection free, and then he was pushing inside her silken walls, taking her completely. "Oh God," she moaned, her hands squeezing her breasts. Her inner walls were still spasming from her orgasm, and he felt his balls tighten. "You're so big. I'm so full."

His hand ran possessively over the slight swell of her stomach. "You said that last time, too," he said, male pride tickling his ego. He pulled back slightly, watching his cock slide out of her ripe pussy, and then pushed in again slowly, watching Anna take him as she moaned. "You're going to come again, sweet Anna," he said, his thumb moving over the soft skin of her sex before he began strumming her clit. "You're going to come with my cock buried inside your body."

Jett began to move faster as his cock swelled even

more. Anna was shaking, her inner walls squeezing him tightly as she bucked up against him. He leaned over her gorgeous body, holding her in place. One hand captured her wrists, holding them in his sure grip. His thumb pressed down against her swollen bud, and as he thrust into her again, she screamed, soaring as he chased down his own release.

He uttered a cry as he came, filling her with his seed. He'd have to clean off the counters after this, but it was worth it. Making love to Anna was always an adventure, and they both loved exploring different places and positions through the house. He'd never look at his kitchen again without seeing Anna naked and sprawled out for his taking.

Jett collected her in his arms afterward, pressing a soft kiss to her lips. Anna was flushed and breathing hard, and he intended to take his time with her tonight after they enjoyed dinner. The house was silent around them, and his lips quirked as he wondered if the nanny had heard Anna's cries of pleasure. No matter. She knew to be discreet. He turned with Anna in his arms, carrying her to the bedroom, letting his gaze fall on her pretty bare breasts. "Let's shower and then eat dinner," he said. "You'll need some sustenance since I plan to keep you busy tonight."

Chapter 3

Jett sat at his laptop the following morning, a smile playing about his lips. He'd taken Anna over and over last night, the memories enough to make his dick twitch. She'd cried out his name so sweetly, he'd wanted to make her come apart repeatedly, his mouth and hands everywhere. He'd risen early to get some work done before he headed into the office, leaving Anna sleeping soundly, her blonde hair spread over the pillow, the sheets covering her naked form. He hadn't heard baby Brody yet and was thankful the nanny had been able to stay the night watching him. While Anna preferred doing everything herself, he loved giving her a break and having some alone time with his fiancée.

His gaze tracked around the kitchen, and he smirked at the mistletoe Anna had hung in the doorway. He'd joked earlier that week that he'd give her a very different kind of kiss beneath it, with his mouth on her delectable pussy.

She'd smiled sweetly and encouraged it—then Brody had started screaming.

Feasting on her last night in the kitchen had been a memory he'd not soon forget. It was different now with a baby in the home, and in a few short years, they'd have young kids running all over the place. He couldn't wait.

The buzzing of his cell phone had him glancing down, and he was surprised to see his brother's name on the screen. Jett swiped the button and lifted the phone to his ear, speaking in a low voice. Although he had an office to work in, he enjoyed sitting in the kitchen most mornings, taking in the silence of the home and view of the trees and forest out back.

"Slate. It's early on the West coast, brother."

"That it is," Slate replied. "I've got a team on the ground I'm monitoring, so I've been on base all night. We've got another hour or so before all hell is about to break loose. I'm waiting on an update from my men. There's no rest for the weary," he quipped.

Jett chuckled. "You love your career, although being in the Navy means you're at the beck and call of Uncle Sam. I take the missions I want and am home when I want. I've got a family to be here for now," he pointed out. Slate didn't seem to mind being single in the least, but Jett enjoyed ribbing him nonetheless.

"How is your better half?" Slate joked. Jett could picture the smirk on his brother's lips. Slate was married to the military, although Anna had sworn that she would set him up one day. How that would happen when they lived on opposite coasts, he wasn't sure, but he wouldn't put anything past her. Anna was determined when she set her mind to something. His brother and Anna had only met twice, but Jett knew she'd charmed him the way she did everyone. It was tough to say no to Anna, a fact he knew all too well. "Did I tell you Anna called me yesterday?" Slate asked.

Jett barked out a laugh. "I knew she was up to something. I got a bit distracted with her last night, but I'll find out what she's up to today. What'd she say?"

"She swore me to secrecy," Slate said, sounding amused. "I'm normally against surprises, but this one was good."

"Damn. I'll get it out of her," Jett promised.

Now it was Slate's turn to laugh. "I doubt it. She's quite determined to keep this one under wraps. She's doing good though?" he asked. "With the pregnancy? She sounded happy."

"She's doing great. Are you ready to be an uncle for the second time?"

"Not at all, but I won't be volunteering for babysitting duty either. Fortunately, the Navy keeps me quite busy."

"Don't I know it." Jett looked up as he heard the sound of a baby crying just then. "Brody just woke up. I better get him since I wanted Anna to sleep in. She's got a sixth sense when it comes to that kid."

"I still can't believe you're a father now," Slate said, but Jett could hear the amusement in his voice. "A fiancée. A new baby. I'm glad you're happy. You deserve it."

"She's good for me, brother," Jett said, repeating what he'd told Slate a year ago when he and Anna had first gotten engaged. Slate had been shocked at the sudden news given that he didn't even know Jett was dating someone. It was quick but absolutely right, and Slate had warmed up to her, as Jett knew he would.

"I can tell. You need someone like Anna to keep you on your toes. Keeps you young," he joked.

Jett's lips quirked. "I have a feeling a houseful of kids will do that to a man. That along with a younger woman."

"She is young, but you work as a couple. Not everyone can handle you, so I give her credit for that. Hope to see you one of these days," Slate said.

"Copy that. Go take care of your SEAL team's business. I've got my own little Army I'm starting here." Jett said goodbye and ended the call, wondering what had prompted that out-of-the-blue chat with Slate. Aside from the tip that Anna had called him last night, Jett still had no idea what his woman was up to. It had to be good if Slate was amused enough to call, he thought with a wry smile.

Damn his brother for not filling him in. No doubt Slate loved knowing something he didn't. Brody's cries continued, and Jett rose from the table, eager to see his child. He'd find out what Anna was up to one way or another, and he couldn't wait.

***

Anna picked up Brody, soothing him as he screamed. Their nanny had already given him a bottle, but the poor thing still hadn't calmed down. "It's all right, baby," she murmured, swaying him back and forth. "You just wanted your mommy." She moved around the nursery, smiling as she sensed Jett at the door. Her skin heated anytime he was near, and that hadn't stopped since becoming a mother.

Last night had been incredible. Jett had made love to her in the steamy shower and then washed every inch of her body, going down on her once more as he declared he'd never get enough of her sweet taste. They'd eaten dinner by candlelight, and when he'd taken her to bed, Jett had thoroughly kissed and caressed every inch of her before taking her in various positions. Anna was deliciously sore and couldn't remember the last time they'd had a night entirely to themselves like that.

"You snuck out of bed early," she chastised, looking at Jett over her shoulder. He looked dark and delicious in the doorway of the nursery, almost too rough and masculine to be in such a sweet space. Almost. Because he doted on her and their child.

His eyes darkened as they tracked over her, taking in the curves concealed beneath her silk robe. "I didn't want to wake you after keeping you up all night."

She shot him a heated look. "You were very thorough."

"I was," he agreed, his voice rich like warm caramel as he moved closer. Soon both Anna and Brody were in his muscular arms, exactly where she wanted to be. "I didn't get here fast enough," he said. "I wanted you to sleep in." His hand landed possessively on her stomach as he kissed her temple. "How are you feeling?" he asked.

"Good. I slept like a baby once you let me rest," she said with a wink. "Well, not our baby. He's a terrible sleeper, but we love you anyway," she cooed.

"Want me to hold him while you shower?"

"Coffee first," she declared. "I sent the nanny home since today is my day off."

"Smart, because what if she caught us with my hands all over you?" Jett asked huskily, letting them roam. Anna still held the baby to her, but his hand slid up from her belly and he palmed one breast, letting his thumb graze over her nipple as he kissed her.

"Mmm," she said. "You can't tease me like that when I'm holding our son."

Jett raised one eyebrow.

"That's like cruel torture," she said as he squeezed her breast gently, kissing her once more before he stepped away.

"Someone's got to make the coffee," he said.

"Yeah, yeah," she mock-grumbled, following him into the hall.

Jett's amused gaze caught hers. "I spoke with my brother this morning," he said nonchalantly.

She stilled, shock coursing through her. "Slate? I'm going to kill him," she muttered. "He promised not to say a word."

"He's a trained Navy SEAL with multiple teams under his command," Jett pointed out. "They're lethal. Killing him would be tough, even for you, sweet Anna."

She shot him a withering look, and Jett chuckled. "Don't worry, he didn't tell me anything. Claimed he was sworn to secrecy or some such nonsense. He just likes goading me," Jett said, shaking his head. "I'll get him back one of these days."

"As you should," Anna agreed.

"Sweetness, I wouldn't let him ruin your surprise," Jett said, sounding amused.

"Yeah right. You love to have the upper hand."

"Exactly. I told him I'd find out myself exactly

what you're up to." He flashed her another look, his eyes twinkling.

"Jett, you would not! You are not going to ruin your Christmas surprise. Promise me you'll behave."

"That I will never promise."

She huffed past him, moving into the kitchen. "You will if you know what's good for you. Now where's this coffee I was promised?"

Jett guided her to a chair, and she could see him biting back a smile as she sank into it with a sleeping Brody still in her arms. Jett ducked down, pressing a soft kiss to her forehead. It was sweet coming from such a gruff, protective man, and she flushed despite herself. Jett was always surprising her, a walking contradiction in many ways, but she loved their life together. Now she'd just need to pull off the surprise of their lives and marry the man of her dreams before Christmas.

Chapter 4

"We've got a problem," Jett said as Luke strode into his office at Shadow Security later that day. Jett dropped the thick file he'd been holding onto his desk, watching as the heavy door swung shut behind Luke.

"The potential mole at DOD you briefed us on the other day?" Luke asked, grabbing a chair in front of Jett's large executive desk.

"Affirmative. The Feds want us to move in, sending West to a government office in Boston where the suspect works. Motherfucker. I needed West on that potential op in Sudan, running the technical side of things. I'll have to get another one of the IT guys on that in case we're sent out soon. My contact with Defense, however, has let me know that the suspected mole is the top priority. We need to find out who's leaking this intelligence and passing it on to our enemies. Although West could probably hack into the DOD systems with the skill set he has, it'd be easier if he's onsite. They're ready to bust this asshole."

"What do you need, boss?" Luke asked.

"Brief the others. I'd like to send one of the team in as well to see what additional information we can find out—get some ears to the ground. We'll be posing as military members on TDY. I've got to meet with West this afternoon to hear his thoughts on the matter. Then I need to find out what Anna's up to," he said, shaking his head.

"Is everything okay?"

"My fiancée is planning a Christmas surprise of sorts, and you know I hate surprises. Even my brother called me this morning about it. He just loves to know something I don't."

"You're kidding me," Luke said with a chuckle.

"Negative. She's up to something, and I intend to find out exactly what. Don't tell Anna. I don't mind playing along, but an actual surprise? Not a chance. I'll figure it out after I deal with this. Decide who wants to spend two weeks in Boston. The rest of the team will potentially have to move in to Sudan."

"We need more guys," Luke assessed.

"That we do, and I've considered expanding. A second Shadow Ops Team would allow us to cover more ground and take additional ops. Hell, my brother commands multiple SEAL teams in Coronado. I think he's even got the Hawaii team under his command on a mission at the moment."

"Wyatt Miller's team?" Luke asked. "He's a good dude. Worked with him once on a joint op back when we were Deltas."

Jett nodded. "I have a feeling his team is deployed

right now. Slate was monitoring something in the middle of the night when he called me with his tip about Anna. Normally, Hawaii doesn't fall under his command, but they've done several joint missions with the Alpha SEALs Coronado teams. There have been some incidents in the Pacific recently."

"I heard," Luke said with a frown. "Hell, I wouldn't mind working with Wyatt again, or any of those guys. Man. Time flies. It's been years since I've seen any of them. It would be good to catch up."

Jett crossed his arms, looking at Luke speculatively.

"I'll let the other Shadow Ops members know we're briefing soon," Luke continued. "If I hear anything about Anna's big surprise, I'll fill you in of course," Luke added.

"You better. Somethings up, and I don't like it."

Luke rose from his seat, and Jett could tell he was biting back a smile. "That woman," Jett muttered. "I'll get it out of her."

"I'm sure you will, boss," Luke said reassuringly. "I'll meet with the team and let you know who's heading to Boston with West. What day are we tasked to start?

"On Monday. Three weeks before Christmas."

"Brody's first Christmas," Luke said with a smile.

"Don't I know it. Anna's already gone overboard buying him a million outfits and toys. While I fully plan to spoil my kids when they're older, he's an infant."

"That's Anna for you. She's clearly enjoyed decorating your office," Luke said, smirking at the colorful lights atop Jett's bookcases and the Santa hat perched on one shelf. His normally organized and neat office had Anna's Christmas touches everywhere.

"Save it," Jett ordered.

"Right. No comment, boss. And as for briefing with the guys on the situation in Boston? I'm on it. Don't worry about a thing."

Jett grumbled as Luke pulled open the door, but then his phone lit up with a text from his pretty fiancée. A feeling of fondness and warmth washed over him. Anna's day off had him missing her more than he'd imagined. Although the nanny wasn't scheduled to come back again this evening, he'd seduce his beautiful fiancée anyway—and find out exactly what she was up to.

***

"Lena, you're such an amazing help," Anna declared, winking at Jett's personal assistant as they sat in the kitchen, organizing a stack of papers and pamphlets. "Remember, not a word to Jett. You've got to promise to keep this a secret."

"Of course," Lena said with a smile. "He didn't even question when I left to run errands earlier. The man's busy enough with his business to run. Of course, if he checks the security cameras of your home, he'll know I've been here for a while," she added ruefully.

"Damn him for being so security conscious," Anna joked, and Lena burst into laughter. She was usually quiet and professional, a get down to business type of person. She'd loosened up a bit over the past year as they'd gotten to know one another better. Anna still recalled the weekend she'd met Jett—and spent several nights at his upstate home. Lena had gone shopping for her since Anna didn't have any clothes, aside from what she'd been wearing at the bar that night. Jett had bought her drinks and dinner, and the rest was history. She and Jett were engaged with a baby. They had another on the way.

She smiled.

"You are positively glowing," Lena declared.

"It's the baby," Anna said, running a hand over her non-existent bump. "I almost can't believe we're about to do this all over again. Jett was so paranoid when I was pregnant the first time. Now he's got both Brody and me to worry about."

"He's protective," Lena said. "There's nothing wrong with that."

"Protective? Absolutely. He's also used to being in charge. He's going to both love and hate that I'm pulling off our wedding without his knowledge," Anna said, giggling. "I can't wait to see his face when I'm standing there in my wedding gown in our backyard. He couldn't care less about the wedding details, per se, and he's more than ready for me to become his wife. Not knowing it's happening in advance will kill him. Jett loves to run the show. I even got his brother on board."

"Slate?" Lena asked, looking impressed. "He's even more stern and serious than Jett, if that's possible."

"Oh, not around me," Anna said, carelessly waving a hand in the air. "I've only met him twice but have made a point to call. He loves our chats, I'm sure." She looked over, noticing Lena smiling in amusement. "I think he gets a kick out of me pulling one over on his brother. He said to tell him the date and he'd be here, come hell or high water."

"They're competitive but close," Lena said. "I can certainly see that he'd want to be here for the big day."

"I guess that competitive gene runs in the family. I wonder if baby Brody will be that way," Anna said with a laugh.

"With Jett as his dad? I'm sure of it," Lena said.

"I'm in so much trouble, aren't I?" Anna asked, shaking her head. "Well, we made some great progress with the plans today. I can't believe you covered so much ground."

"I didn't mind going in person to vet some of the vendors. Everyone has websites and social media nowadays, but I got a real feel for them. A business can put up a fancy website, but I want to make sure they actually have the skills we need."

"Good call. I don't want people who are going to flake out on us at the last minute or promise they do weddings all the time but can't handle a crowd—or worse, promise to cater and then reheat frozen meals. I read a story about that somewhere. The vendor was just reheating frozen food from the grocery store."

"Who was this?" Lena asked with a laugh.

"Some food truck. Honestly, I think it was a group of college guys trying to make some money. Anyway, not that I don't love me a good food truck, but I want to go a little fancier for my wedding day. Plus, given the short notice, we'll be limited as to which vendors are available. Between coordinating with a caterer and bartender, it sounds like we'll have to do a Friday evening, at least based on the places we've contacted."

"It'll be perfect. And as for the people flying in, they'd be here for the weekend anyway," Lena assured her. "If we can estimate a headcount, I'll get tables and chairs reserved. Linens, too. I think the caterer has place settings, but I'll confirm before we sign the contract."

"Contracts with vendors? This is getting real. Ohhh, this is so exciting!" Anna squealed. "I wanted to nail down the date and the specifics for the biggest things today. I'll have to go dress shopping this week too of course. Shoot! What do you think Jett will want to wear? He'll need a tux, unless he wants his military uniform."

"Leave Jett to me," Lena assured her. "I'll make sure he has the appropriate attire for his own wedding. The only thing he'll have to worry about is how incredible you look."

"Eeek! You're the best!" Anna said, leaning over and throwing her arms around the other woman's shoulders.

"What about rings?" Lena asked.

"Oh, we already have those. We were actually going to start planning before I got pregnant—the first time," Anna added wryly. "Jett will be so shocked, because I was insistent that I didn't want to wear a wedding dress while pregnant."

"You're not even showing."

"Exactly. We could've had it last year, but eh?" She shrugged. "We had our time as a couple during the pregnancy without worrying about wedding planning. I was sicker that go around, too. This time, I feel great." Anna rose and walked over to the bassinet, where baby Brody was sleeping peacefully. "I swear this kid can sleep through anything during the day. I just need to get him on board with sleeping at night."

"He'll get there," Lena said.

Anna looked at her thoughtfully. Lena wasn't much older than her, probably in her early thirties. She didn't know much about the other woman despite the many hours they'd spent together. Lena kept her private life private. "Do you want kids?" Anna asked.

"No. I love children but never pictured myself having any of my own."

"What about a boyfriend?" Anna asked.

Lena shook her head. "Don't get any matchmaker ideas in your head. I'm busy and happy as a single woman."

"I hear ya. If Jett hadn't taken me home from that bar in Manhattan, I'd still be single, too."

"He was smitten with you from day one," Lena said.

"He didn't stand a chance," Anna said with a wink. "And he's going to be shocked as anything when I pull off our wedding without his knowledge. Okay," she said, looking down at her notes. "I still need to decide on flowers, shoes, and the dress. Oh my God, and the cake! How could I forget about that?"

Lena smiled, sliding several more brochures toward her. "I took the liberty of checking out some local bakeries this morning as well. We can schedule a tasting if you'd like."

"Perfect! Yes, let's get that on the schedule ASAP. I'll call Ashleigh and Jen to bring them up to speed. Even though we're rushing the wedding, I still want to go dress shopping in Manhattan. I'll have to buy something off the rack, but that's fine. Oh shoot—I can't even drink the champagne those boutiques offer when you schedule a session to look at dresses. Well, maybe just a sip," she said. "I'll bring my own sparkling cider or something."

"What else do you need me to do?" Lena asked, looking amused.

"Get the contracts for the caterer and bartender. I'll sign off after I look them over so we have that in writing. I've got a lead on an officiant, so that should work as well. I'm going to finalize the guest list this afternoon. Luckily, we'd already discussed who we'd invite, so he can't be upset about that."

"I don't think that man could be upset with you about anything," Lena said.

Anna lifted a shoulder. "He loves me."

"Without a doubt. Want me to order wedding invitations?" Lena asked. "I can do a rush order."

"Huh," Anna said, pondering. "I was planning to text invitations tonight. Maybe that can be a save the date type of thing. Obviously, I'll tell people it's a surprise and under no circumstances should they fill in Jett about what's happening. Then we'll do the invitations as more of a formality."

"Yes, I think that would be nice."

"We are off to an amazing start," Anna said. "Jett's pretty convinced I've got this secret Christmas gift up my sleeve. He's got no clue about what's really happening."

"Well, I don't blame him for thinking it's a Christmas gift. You've gone all out with the decorating. The house looks good," Lena said.

"You don't think it's too many trees?" Anna asked. "I love the small one in the foyer. Obviously, we needed a big one in the living room to put all the gifts from Santa. And the tree on the deck is perfect. It's so romantic to sit out there at night under the stars and look at the twinkling lights."

Lena rose from her chair, smiling. "I never in a million years would've dreamed Jett would have Christmas decorations overflowing his home. It's warmer now with you here."

"It just needed a woman's touch," Anna declared.

"For certain," Lena said, crossing over to look out the back doors onto the deck. "Now you're not really planning to have the wedding outside, are you? December in New York?"

"Of course, I am. We'll rent a giant tent with heaters or something for the dinner. Oh, add that to the list," she said, watching as Lena walked back over to the table and jotted it down. "It'll be so romantic. I'll have a warm wrap or something to go over the dress. We'll tell everyone to wear a coat. The ceremony will be short and sweet, but with the tent, we'll be fine for dinner and dancing. We can always move into the house if it gets too cold."

"I'll make note of that for the caterers. Your home is large enough, but the backyard is certainly beautiful."

"I've been plotting for a while," Anna said. "Jett's so busy all the time anyway, what with running things at Shadow Security, he doesn't need to worry about wedding details."

"We're off to a good start."

"We'll reconvene later this week," Anna said. "I'll send you the guest list, too. You don't mind sending the invitations out?"

"Not at all. I'll do a rush order and get the invitations in the mail. Don't worry about a thing."

"You really are the best," Anna said, giving her another quick hug.

"I don't mind a new challenge," Lena said. "Being

Jett's personal assistant has come with all sorts of random tasks over the years. This takes the cake," she joked.

"Of course. He could never outwit me," Anna said with a giggle.

Chapter 5

Jett drummed his fingers on the conference table, frowning. "This doesn't look good, boss," Nick said, eyeing the surveillance footage from outside the DOD building. They watched as a man looked left and right, seemingly trying to determine if anyone was around. He clutched the messenger bag he was carrying tightly, then turned and hurried toward the parking lot in the distance.

"Not at all," Sam drawled. "What the hell is that guy doing snooping around the perimeter? Doesn't he realize there are cameras all over the place?"

"He's young and dumb," Gray said. "Of course, that works to our advantage."

Jett shook his head, pausing the video. He clicked on the computer, pulling up the picture of a DOD badge with a photo and name. "Peter Susco is a contractor with DOD. He's worked in the Boston office for two years but has recently fallen on financial troubles. He has a high-level clearance, granting him access to Top Secret, compartmented information. While my contact at DOD has a list of people with access to the materials that have been leaked online, Peter Susco's recent activity has aroused suspicions."

"He's hidden his tracks fairly well," West said. "His electronic trail, at any rate. The IT staff said it looked like everyone in Susco's branch was pulling all the files in question. He was able to alter the records showing who accessed the data. It looked like everyone on his team accessed the documents every hour. Potentially, it would incriminate everyone."

"And you have a solution for this?" Jett asked.

"I just need to get on his actual machine. If he's involved in leaking the classified information like we suspect, I'll be able to prove it to the Feds."

"And wrap up this case in a neat little package," Jett quipped.

"What about everyone else in his branch?" Nick asked. "They'll wonder why you're on his machine and no one else's."

"We'll swap them out," West said. "I'll have the IT staff put a new stack of CPUs at Peter Susco's workstation."

"How many computers does the guy have?" Ford asked in confusion.

"He has access to multiple networks," West explained. "Each one has a separate CPU for security. He's logging in with his credentials. Many of those government cubicles are set up the same way. Anyone with access can log in to any workstation under their own ID and password."

"I don't know," Nick said, frowning. "You'd think

this would make him suspicious. If he's a computer guy, he'd probably realize the actual computers are different."

"Which is why you'll be there with a cover story," Jett said. "Both of you are TDY to that office. Get a feel for what's going on. We'll have IT set up a temporary workstation for Nick. They'll be moving equipment around, so he won't have reason to question it. Then maybe West can show the technical staff there a new trick or two so we can nail this asshole down."

"He's good," West said. "I'm not surprised they were having trouble figuring it out. I think I know what he did though, I just need to get onto his machine to prove it."

"He might be good with computers, but apparently he's lacking common sense," Gray said, glancing at a picture on the screen. "Stealthy, he's not. He's sneaking around the building like he didn't know he was being watched."

Jett shook his head. "It appears that he's one of those book smart, not street smart type of guys. He'd make a piss poor operator."

"I doubt he'd pass bootcamp, boss," Sam said with a smirk.

"So was he taking physical or electronic copies from the building?" Nick asked. "The way he's looking around makes me wonder what's in that messenger bag."

"Both, which is another problem," Jett said. "The IT staff should've been notified right away if he attached hardware to his computer or inserted a flash drive. It never should've gotten to this point."

"He's managed to fly under the radar, disguising

his actions, but I'll get him," West said.

"And I'll get a feel for what's going on in that office to make sure no one else is involved," Nick said.

"Looks like he did himself in with that surveillance footage," Gray said.

"That tipped off security. He and the others in his branch were already under suspicion for the leaked materials. He's the only one with financial troubles, however. We'll get in there and wrap this case up." Jett clapped his hands together and rose from the table, moving to grab a stack of files. "Now that we've discussed Boston, let's look at Sudan. The rest of the team may be moving in soon to clean up that mess."

***

Hours later, Jett entered the code to disable the alarm of his home and turned the doorknob, walking into his foyer. Anna had been home all day with the baby, but she'd texted him to say he was down for the night. Or for a few hours at least, Jett thought wryly. Brody certainly hadn't started sleeping through the night yet.

His eyes tracked to the living room, and he smiled as he saw the Christmas tree lighting up the otherwise formal space. Anna had gone overboard with decorating, with garland and mistletoe throughout the home and multiple trees, but that was just her. She was exuberant and over-the-top. Fun. Life with her had been an adventure from day one, and he'd missed her today when stuck in back-to-back briefings at headquarters.

"Hey baby," Anna said as he walked into the kitchen. She was washing baby bottles at the sink, and he did a double-take as he set his things down on the table. The scene was so damn domestic yet somehow suited her. Anna was a natural at everything—running a home, being a new mom, keeping things operating smoothly at the office. Even her old firm had begged her to return when she'd left her job on Wall Street. She was an asset to anything she did.

"Hi sweetness," he said, moving across the room. She had on leggings with a white tee shirt, and as Anna glanced over at him, he realized she wasn't wearing a bra. Her nipples pressing against the soft cotton was an erotic sight. Even in casual clothes, Anna was a knockout. Sexy and sweet at the same time. His cock twitched, and he moved closer to give her a gentle kiss. Her hands were still in the soapy water, and he wrapped his hands around her hips, holding her in place as his lips moved leisurely over hers.

"Mmmm," she murmured as the kiss grew heated, one of his hands tangling in her hair. She turned and lifted her soapy hands to his face, cupping it with a smile. He rubbed the scruff of his jaw against her soapy hands, and her eyes danced with amusement. "Did you miss me?" she asked as Jett pulled back, chuckling.

He grabbed a towel from the counter, scrubbing it over his face. "All day. I had nonstop meetings, but I was tempted to sneak out early."

"Whatever for?" she teased with a wink.

"Just anxious to see my fiancée," he said, his eyes raking over her again. Anna's nipples had pebbled with their heated kiss, and he moved closer, nipping at her neck, one hand lightly grazing her breast through the cotton of her shirt.

"What's in the bag?" she asked, catching sight of it as he nuzzled against her soft skin.

"Just some Christmas things," he said, his lips at her ear. "No peeking," he chastised as she tried to move toward it. Jett caught her in his arms, smirking. "If you can keep surprises, then so can I. I saw Lena was here earlier."

"Checking the security cameras, were you? Well, no worries. She stopped by to visit when running some errands, but I have her sworn to secrecy."

"She's on my payroll," Jett said dryly.

Anna scoffed and turned back to the sink, quickly rinsing the remaining bottles. "You wouldn't dare try to get it out of her. Besides, us women know how to stick together. You should know that by now."

"Learned it from the best," he quipped.

Anna looked over her shoulder, the amusement clear on her face. "That you did. Who says you can't teach an old dog new tricks?" Jett tried to choke back his laughter as Anna's phone began buzzing on the counter. Although he was fifteen years older than her, their age difference had never been an issue. She was young. Vibrant. And Anna had captured his interest like no woman ever had before.

"It's Ashleigh," Jett said as he glanced at Anna's phone.

"Oh, put it on speaker!" Anna replied, swishing the water around in the last bottle before dumping it out.

"Hey hun!" Anna said as Jett set the phone near her on the counter. "I'm just getting ready to sterilize some bottles. Jett's here," she quickly added.

"Hi Jett! How's the whole saving the world thing going? Do you miss me yet?"

"Hi Ashleigh," he said, resisting the urge to smile. "Of course, I miss all of Anna's friends. You should come up from the city one weekend." Anna frequently put her friends on speakerphone when she was talking with them. It was amusing to listen in on their conversations. He'd even offered some advice once or twice, although her friends sometimes found it hard to believe that impulsive, headstrong Anna was the one who'd settled down first. "How's life in Brooklyn?" he asked.

"Good. Just working on another book that I'm publishing next year."

"Ah, of course. A writer's gotta write."

"Something like that," Ashleigh said with a laugh. "If I'm not reading, I'm writing. Or trying to understand Anna's cryptic texts."

Anna quickly reached over and snatched the phone, taking it off speaker. She shooed Jett away, moving out onto the back deck. He watched her in amusement from inside the kitchen. Apparently Slate, Ashleigh, and Lena all knew Anna's Christmas surprise. He shook his head. His woman was something else. He could listen to the outside security camera feed if he really wanted to find out what was going on, but Jett wasn't about to go that far. Anna seemed to enjoy the idea of surprising him. If he teased it out of her in other ways, so be it. He wouldn't snoop on her electronically.

She shivered slightly as she spoke on the phone, and he grabbed the coat he'd tossed on the kitchen table. The moonlight shone down on her, the deck and patio area lit up from the twinkling lights of the

Christmas tree outside. He wasn't exactly a romantic, but something about her out there seemed magical. Jett grabbed the baby monitor and opened the doors to the deck, smirking as she quickly ended the call.

Jett shut the door behind him as she set down her phone, his eyes heating as he looked at her. "You looked cold," he murmured.

"So you brought the baby monitor out here to warm me up?" she joked.

Jett set the monitor on the table and wrapped his coat around her, pressing a kiss to her forehead as she shivered. "I brought myself out here to warm you up. Is all this cloak and dagger really necessary?" he asked, eyeing her phone.

"Absolutely. You'll just have to learn to be patient," she said.

"That's tough around you. It's safe for you to use the hot tub now, right?" he asked. Normally Jett was a man of action, used to taking charge, but he'd found himself uncertain more than once during her pregnancy. He wanted his hands and mouth all over her, making her cry out his name, but he wanted to soothe and care for her, too. Tend to all her needs.

Her eyes lit up at the mention of the hot tub. "Yes, but only for ten minutes or so. You'll have to be quick," she teased. "Think you're up for the challenge?" she asked lightly.

Jett's gaze raked over her. Her breasts were pressed against the white cotton of her tee shirt, her nipples hard. Anna's long, blonde hair blew gently in the night breeze, and he wanted to simply devour her. "That's never a problem with you around. I'm hard all the time," he said, his voice gravel. He pressed closer, his lips at her ear. "And you're so sensitive, I can always make you come quickly. I'll take my time later when I have you in bed."

"Promise?"

He chuckled, moving in for a heated kiss before he guided her over to the hot tub, flipping on the jets. His gaze landed on the lounge chairs where he'd first held Anna a year ago, her naked body pinned against him as he made her come apart in his arms. She'd been responsive and enthusiastic even then, mere hours after they'd met in Manhattan.

And he'd spent the entire weekend making her his.

Jett grabbed towels from the outside storage cabinet, thankful he'd thought to put two plush robes there. Anna was already stripping, and his cock twitched. She'd never been shy around him, happy to have his gaze on her gorgeous body. Her breasts bounced enticingly as she lifted her shirt above her head, and then Jett was on her, palming her breasts and stripping off her leggings. He wanted to feast on her, tasting every delicious inch, but it was freezing outside. Jett helped her into the water, listening to her giggles. The contrast between the bite of the cold winter air and hot, bubbling water was always startling. Sensual. He loved nothing more than spending alone time with Anna out here.

Jett quickly shucked off his own clothes, ignoring the cold and instead watching as her body disappeared beneath the swirling water, a playful smile on her lips. Anna's long, blonde hair floated around her, giving her an almost ethereal look. "You're a siren," he murmured. "Sexy and sweet and too damn tempting for me to ever resist."

He stepped into the water, his cock already hard, watching as she teasingly moved away. Jett growled and pulled Anna onto his lap as she laughed, enjoying the feel of her wet, warm body against his own. He shifted her so she was straddling him, her full breasts pillowed against his chest, her ass nestled atop his stiff cock. Their lips clashed, hungry and desperate, and then his hands were everywhere—palming her breasts, teasing her nipples, sliding between her pussy lips to feel her silken arousal

"Jett," she breathed, clinging to him as he toyed with her clit.

"You're going to come for me, sweetness. Come on my fingers and then on my cock." He shifted her higher, easing two fingers inside her molten core. Anna gasped as he urged her on, pinning her against him with one muscular arm. "That's right, honey. Come for me." His thumb slid over her clit, rubbing in circles.

"Jett," she wailed, head falling onto his shoulder.

"You're even more sensitive now," he said, nipping at the softness of her neck. "Come on my fingers, sweet Anna. Give yourself to me."

Anna's entire body tightened, her pussy clenching tightly around him, and then as he worked his hand faster, rubbing her clit, she cried out his name, clinging to him in the cold winter night. Anna was still gasping and pleading as he eased her back down from her shuddering orgasm, her face flushed, her body ripe and ready for him. Jett shifted her once more, lining her pussy up with his thick erection. Her slender thighs were spread around him, her cleavage rising above the water, tempting him. "Are you ready to take me, sweetness?"

"Yes. I need you."

He gripped her hips as she lined herself up, and

then the head of his swollen cock notched at her entrance. She whimpered, the hot tub bubbling around them, and then Jett thrust into her in one quick movement. Anna gasped, her inner walls pulsing around him, and he held himself in place, trying to remain in control. "You feel so good," he murmured. His hands slid to her ass, gripping, and her breasts rose above the bubbling water as she shifted up.

"Ride me," he ordered. And then she was, Jett's big hands squeezing her bottom possessively as Anna shifted her hips, taking what she needed. He ducked, sucking a pretty nipple into his mouth as she cried out at the new sensation. Her fingernails scratched his head, the bite of pain welcome. Jett loved nothing more than driving her out of her mind. His balls tightened as she squeezed him with her pussy, and then he took over, needing to make her come once more.

Jett's hands wrapped around her hips and pulled Anna down as he thrust up. Anna's cry came out of nowhere, her orgasm forcing his own. Her inner walls milked him, and Jett felt his balls tightening more before he exploded. "Anna!" he ground out, holding her to him as his cock twitched again, still buried deep inside her body. They were both breathing heavily as he kissed her sweetly, softer than before. "I love you," he murmured.

"I love you too, baby."

"Let's get you back inside," he said, reluctantly shifting her off him so he could grab a towel and robe for her. Ignoring the cold himself with only a quick, efficient toweling off, he wrapped her in a fluffy robe as she stepped out of the hot tub and lifted her into his arms.

"I can walk," she teased as he carried her across the deck.

"But then I don't get to hold you close," he said. The cries of Brody on the baby monitor had both their eyes shifting to the table. "I'll get him," Jett said. "You go get warmed up and relax."

"Have I mentioned that I love you?" she asked as he set her down carefully in the kitchen.

Jett's lips quirked as he shut the back door, setting the alarm. "You might have, but I don't mind hearing it again. Go," he said, playfully nudging her toward their bedroom. "I'll be in after I take care of baby Brody. I'm not done with you yet," he added with a wink.

Chapter 6

"He looks worried," Anna said Monday afternoon, watching as Jett rushed down the hall to the conference room. Luke was at his side, and they were talking rapidly about something in low voices.

"Yeah. Some of the team is gone," Clara pointed out. "Nick and West are on assignment. It's unusual for West to be gone for an extended amount of time. Usually, he's here at headquarters or attending local meetings. I wonder what this is about."

"You'd think December would be more petty theft at retailers, not secret government-sanctioned missions," Anna said wryly. "Jett said we'd be busy this week dealing with several situations. I already had to order some supplies in case some of the team goes overseas. I'm pretty sure Nick and West are stateside. Jett seemed preoccupied all weekend. I almost felt bad leaving Brody with him. I couldn't tell him why I'd gone into the city, so the timing wasn't ideal."

"I'm sure he figured you were just Christmas shopping with your friends," Clara assured her. "After all, it is baby's first Christmas."

"You're right. Besides, Jett insisted that I deserved a chance to relax and catch up with my girlfriends." Anna shot her a smug look. "The man had no clue I was trying on wedding dresses."

"And the one you sent me a picture of was beautiful."

"It was incredible, wasn't it? It practically fit like a glove," Anna said with a smile. "And oh my goodness, I almost forgot how amazing Manhattan is at Christmas. I lived there for years, so I should know. We really don't get into the city much anymore with a new baby."

"Things will change," Clara assured her.

"Well, not anytime soon," Anna declared, rubbing her flat stomach.

"Give it a few years then," Clara said. "You'll be pushing the double stroller down the streets of Manhattan. Or not," she added with a grin. "You've got a nanny, so grab your guy and go."

"I should. Jett and I met in Manhattan, after all. We could use an amazing date night there. Speaking of the city, I've got to call Ashleigh," Anna said. "The bridal boutique was able to take measurements for alterations on the gown I picked out. It was almost perfect, but they were going to tweak a few little things. Ashleigh's going to head back to the bridal shop to pick it up for me so I don't have to make another trip."

"You're lucky to have such great friends."

"I miss them sometimes, living upstate," Anna admitted. "I wouldn't change my life with Jett and

Brody for anything, but my girlfriends and I sure had fun when we were younger."

"Didn't we all," Clara agreed with a laugh. "Well, some of us more than most," she added, looking at Anna pointedly.

"Guilty as charged," Anna joked.

"Life is good now," Clara said. "Better."

"It's a thousand times better. Hey, do you want to taste test some wedding cakes with me this week? Lena is going to set up an appointment for me at a few local bakeries. I obviously can't bring Jett since it's a surprise."

"For sure," Clara said. "Can they bake a wedding cake with short notice?"

"We'll find out," Anna said with a shrug. "If not, we'll have fancy cupcakes or something. A donut cake," she said as inspiration struck. "That's going to be my backup plan. The point is to marry my man and surprise the hell out of him. He'll walk into the backyard and not even know what's coming."

"I'll be extremely impressed if you manage to pull this off without Jett finding out. He knows everything."

"That's why this wedding will be so amazing. He's fully expecting us to wait another year until baby number two arrives. But guess what? We've waited long enough, so this mission is a go. His brother already requested leave and booked a flight to New York."

"Slate's really coming? I've heard about him over the years but never met the man. He sounds more intimidating than Jett."

"For sure," Anna agreed. "Slate's a real hard ass. He's been in the military his entire career. We'll have other men in uniform there, too. The Shadow Ops guys are helping me reach out to some old Army buddies of Jett's. They should be coming as far as I know. My parents are flying in. My best friends are already here in New York."

"And you know most everyone in the office is coming, aside from the essential staff needed to keep headquarters running."

"Maybe I should live stream the wedding ceremony," Anna mused.

"That's smart. Are you hiring a videographer?"

"Oh shit. I should. I need a photographer, too," Anna said, biting her lip. "How could I forget about that? I swear, pregnancy brain is a real thing. Quick, start googling names of local photographers. I can't believe that wasn't even on my list. We need to hurry before Jett comes out here and sees what we're up to."

***

Jett sat back in his office, watching the surveillance footage on his large monitors. West had set up a secure feed for him to see what was happening inside the Defense Department building. Although cameras weren't allowed inside of SCIFs, also known as sensitive compartmented information facilities, the unclassified areas of the office were fair game. The cameras were discreet and would be unnoticeable to most. The higher ups knew what was going on, but Peter Susco and the rest of the employees were left in the dark.

While this wasn't the type of operation that Jett would normally have eyes on, he was curious about the man leaking classified intel. He'd already been noticed walking suspiciously around the office building. It made little sense, because if Susco had stolen information on a flash drive, he could've hidden it easily on his person, walking out of the building with no one the wiser. Peter Susco seemed to also be taking hardcopies of various intelligence reports. Once they found them, they'd have both an electronic and paper trail—the electronic fingerprints from when he'd accessed the files, and the hard copies that he'd evidently printed out. They just needed to prove Susco was the only person involved.

The camera had only been in there one day, and Jett watched as Susco stacked various reports on his desk. That alone was a security breach, because all classified materials should've remained in the SCIF.

"This guy can't be this dumb," Jett muttered.

Luke poked his head in the door. "What was that, boss?"

Jett's gaze flicked to him then back to his screen. "Just watching the footage from Boston. It's almost like this asshole wants to be caught."

"Except he covered his tracks electronically," Luke pointed out. "His entire team has allegedly accessed every single report that was leaked. We know that's bullshit, and Susco is likely behind it. West will be able to prove that while he's onsite."

"Affirmative. I'm not sure what Susco's endgame is. He had to realize snooping around outside the office building would make people suspicious. It almost seems like he's trying to draw attention to himself."

"Any updates from West?"

Jett shook his head. "Nothing yet. The IT guys will

be swapping out the CPUs tonight—routine maintenance as far as anyone else is concerned. Nick's getting a feel for the office, talking to people. We don't want a full-blown interrogation, just an idea of what others might know. The Feds will deal with Susco after we gather enough on him. West will get his hands on the computers at oh-four-hundred tomorrow. Even though the DOD staff couldn't find the electronic fingerprints left by Susco, I have no doubt West will. Once we can prove Susco is behind the breach, we can wrap this operation up."

"I'm surprised they're still letting him have access to the office building and secure servers," Luke said with a frown.

"It wasn't my call. It's a risk, but he's been leaking information for several months, and they want to catch him red-handed. DOD narrowed down a list of suspects as the flow of classified intel grew. Lives are in danger because of this asshole. Why he's purposefully getting sloppy now is problematic. He's up to something."

"Maybe he's in over his head and wants to get out."

"By ending up in jail? He's leaking more intelligence."

"It's a busy time of year," Luke said. "Maybe he needed cash to pay for the holidays. He needs more money and is selling more secrets."

Jett raised his eyebrows, and Luke held up both hands, chuckling. "I'm just saying it can get expensive. Christmas," he added, almost as if an afterthought.

Jett let out a groan. "Anna was teasing me all weekend about her big Christmas surprise. I don't suppose you know anything about it?"

"I'm sworn to secrecy, boss. It's good though."

Jett shook his head. "I was out in the lobby earlier and heard Anna and Clara conspiring. I'm pretty sure the whole damn building knows what's going on and not me. Obviously, I could pull the camera feeds and find out for myself, but she's so damn excited, I don't want to ruin it for her."

"You've got it bad," Luke joked with a grin as he crossed his arms.

"I'd do anything for her," Jett admitted.

"I hope you're talking about me!" Anna trilled, peeking her head around the open doorway, a huge smile on those plush lips. Her wrap dress swished with the movement, and Jett's hungry gaze raked over her, taking in the way it hugged her breasts and skimmed over her hips. "Oh hi, Luke. Hope you weren't giving away my big secret."

"Of course not. Wren and I are both like vaults," he said, pretending to zip his lips shut and toss away the key.

"Jesus," Jett muttered, running a hand over his face. "Even your women know?"

"Yep," Luke said, looking amused.

"I knew I could count on you," Anna told him. "I think my fiancé is starting to realize everyone knows my Christmas surprise but him. This is kind of fun," she teased. Anna brushed past Luke as she sashayed across Jett's office like she owned the place, draping herself over his lap and kissing his cheek.

Luke's lips quirked. "It sure the hell is fun," he agreed, winking at Anna. "And on that note, I'm out. I'll be on standby if you get any more info on the overseas mission," he told Jett, his smile fading.

"Otherwise, I'll catch you both tomorrow."

Jett nodded goodbye before he clicked off the surveillance footage on his computer screen and then properly kissed Anna hello, taking her sweet mouth with his own. His hands tangled in her hair, and she melted against him, wrapping her arms around his neck.

"That looked positively boring to watch," she said, her eyes shining with amusement as they finally broke their heated kiss. Jett's erection was pressing against her bottom, and he knew she could feel it. Anna licked her lips, and he had to stop himself from kissing her again.

"It was, but it can't be helped. Just trying to catch the bad guy," Jett said dryly.

"That's where West and Nick are this week," she said astutely. As much as she loved to flirt and tease him, not much slipped by Anna. She wasn't involved in any of their operations, but she was sharp. He'd do anything and everything in his power to protect her from the darkness in his line of work. Her efficiency and organization helped keep the black ops side of his business running smoothly, but she'd never be involved in any dangerous tasks.

"They are. I'm hoping to end this in a matter of days though. We've got other missions coming up, and I need the team ready."

"Well, as long as everyone plays nice after that. I can't have them ruining my Christmas surprise."

Jett's lips quirked. "I was thinking," he said, letting his hands roam over Anna's gorgeous body. She was facing him, away from the door to his office, and he palmed one breast, listening to her tiny whimper. His cock twitched, and he wished he could take her right here, sinking into her tight heat and making her cry out his name. "We should get away for a couple nights around Christmas. Have the nanny watch Brody. I want some time alone together."

Anna's eyes lit up with delight.

"You like that idea." It wasn't a question. He shifted the fabric of her wrap dress, exposing her lacy bra. "I should've told Luke to close the door to the office," he muttered, glaring at the opening.

She giggled, watching his movements. Jett's fingers trailed over the fabric hugging her cleavage, and he tugged it lower, exposing her nipple. His thumb swiped over the pink bud, watching as it tightened. Anna playfully swatted at him, and he righted her bra and dress, grumbling. "No, you shouldn't have, because we're at work," Anna pointed out. "I'm not opposed to quickies, as you're well aware," she teased, "but I've got stuff to do this afternoon. Clara and I have an errand to run when she finishes with those numbers she's pulling."

"And you have work here to do," he said regretfully.

"Yep. I have several things to finish up. And if I spend too much time in here with the boss, I won't be able to finish them in order to sneak out. You said you'd be home a bit late tonight, so I figured it was a good time to run our, ahem, errand."

Jett lifted a hand, his fingers trailing down her cheek until he was cupping her jaw. "And this errand is about my Christmas present?" he asked, his voice gruff.

"Maybe," she teased.

"Anna," he said, his lips pressing against her slender neck as she arched against him. "I have my ways of finding out what you're up to." His other hand trailed up her spine, and he didn't miss the way she shivered in delight.

"Of course, you do," she said, smiling before sliding off his lap. She glanced down, making sure her breasts were properly covered, and Jett's hands itched to pull her close once again. "But I also know you wouldn't dare. Don't ruin your surprise, baby."

"Maybe I'll get it out of you tonight," he said, his lips quirking. "Tease you until you can't say no."

"You could try," she said, winking at him. "Finish your surveillance stuff."

He shook his head, trying to hide his smile. "So that was a yes for a getaway at Christmas? I'll look into booking something or have Lena plan it for us."

"As long as it's after Christmas. Brody's first Christmas needs to be at home. And let's go someplace tropical. A beach vacation! That sounds heavenly, doesn't it? You, me, sunscreen, fruity drinks—virgin for me, of course. You'll sip your whiskey; I'll have a virgin pina colada. It'll be heavenly."

"I'll have you all to myself," he said, his blood heating.

"Maybe I'll blindfold you this time," she joked. "It sounds perfect, baby. I'll stop in before I leave for the day. Don't stay too late."

His phone began to buzz on his desk, and she blew him a kiss before turning to leave. Jett watched Anna's hips sway as she sauntered out of his office, her dress swishing around her shapely legs. His Anna was a temptress. It was amusing to watch her try to keep her secret from him, but he wouldn't have it any other way. Jett might control things in the bedroom, taking her how he wanted, but they both knew Anna was really the one who had the upper hand.

Chapter 7

Anna giggled as she drove home later that week, her phone on speaker. "Ash, I wish you could've been there yesterday. The cakes we tasted were to die for. Sinful. I swear, I almost orgasmed on the spot."

She could hear her friend choking back laughter on the other end of the line. "Orgasmic cakes? Now that is impressive. Please tell me that's the one you picked for your wedding."

"Of course," Anna said, biting back a smile. "Wasn't that obvious from my description?"

"I wonder what the guests will think," Ashleigh joked. "Don't the bride and groom get the first taste? Sounds like it will be quite a show."

"That's why you love me," Anna said in a sing-song voice. "Think of how boring life would be if I wasn't around. Maybe it's the pregnancy hormones making me crazy." She flicked on her turn signal and got in the right lane, exiting onto the street that led to their neighborhood. Jett had a huge, sprawling property that backed up to the woods. The perimeter was secured by a fence and surveillance cameras, along with a gated entry, so it was private and safe. It would be perfect for their wedding day.

"I hope you leave that bakery a fabulous review. Maybe I will too after your wedding," Ashleigh said.

"I'm telling you, it was amazing. I selected the design of the cake, too. It'll be a white cake of course, but I want some deep red flowers on top. It'll be Christmassy enough to match the décor but still look like a wedding cake. I'm going to have our landscaping guys put up thousands of little twinkling lights out back—Christmas lights. They'll have to do some of that in advance, but I'm telling Jett it's just more decorations for the holidays. I'm always extravagant and over-the-top, so he won't think anything of it."

She heard Ashleigh's huff of laughter. "Aside from the lights you're putting up in the backyard, Jett seriously has no idea what's going on?"

"He thinks I'm planning some big Christmas surprise," Anna admitted. "A gift or something. He knows something is up but has absolutely no idea about the wedding. The extra decorating doesn't even faze him. Did I tell you I strung lights in his office at work?"

"At Shadow Security? That must be something else."

"I think he secretly loves it. No one ever doted on him before. He's gruff and no-nonsense. All business. That's why he has me," Anna said confidently. "We balance each other out."

"That you do. We need someone to bring you

back down to earth sometimes," Ashleigh teased. "You moved out of the city, so that's Jett's job now."

"Ha. The man doesn't mind it one bit."

"Not at all. He's smitten with you. I was surprised last week when I saw your text about the wedding," Ashleigh admitted. "It's just like you to pull off something like this though. Impulsive and crazy but kind of practical in its own way, too. Check that wedding off your list."

"Exactly, girl. We've put it off for a year already. He knocked me up again. The man has super sperm or something."

Ashleigh laughed over the phone. "He must be extremely virile. All that raw masculinity has to be channeled into something."

"Things in the bedroom are good," Anna admitted. "I swear I can't get enough of him. And as for making Jett my husband? We might as well move things along."

"Only you, Anna. I have to admit, I kind of enjoy knowing a secret Jett doesn't. The man will be floored when he sees you standing there in a wedding gown."

"That's the plan," Anna said with a laugh. "He was pretty much ready to marry me on the spot the weekend we met."

"Did he have a choice?" Ashleigh joked. "You went home with him and basically never left."

"Don't I know it. Someday we'll tell our kids that story," she mused. "Well, I'll leave out the R-rated parts of course. Luckily Brody is sleeping in the backseat and too young to understand anyway. Let's just say I was deliciously sore after that first night."

"It was love at first sight," Ashleigh said. "Just like some of the couples I write about. Well, I do enjoy a good love-hate story, too."

"How's the new book coming along?" Anna asked.

"It's good! Somewhat ironic that I write sexy romances when I'm single, but that's life."

"You'll meet someone," Anna insisted. "I'll set you up."

"Don't you dare."

Anna smirked. There was absolutely no way she was promising that. "We'll see. Are you writing this afternoon?"

"I will be. I'm just taking a break right now."

"I'm still not used to this part-time schedule at the office but have to admit I don't mind having the afternoon to run errands. Jett's swamped with several jobs at work and has been getting home late, so it gives me even more time alone on my days off. He's stressed, but I've got a wedding to plan. It gives him less time to figure out what I'm up to."

"He works hard. That's the danger of running your own security firm, I suppose."

"He hired me to take on some extra work, and what happened? I go on maternity leave less than a year later and come back part-time. He actually wanted me to stay home with the baby. Jett knows how much I adore Brody, but I wasn't ready to give up the office completely. Now after the second baby comes? Who knows. I might be momming it up full time then."

"Probably so. You're an amazing mom. I've got no idea how you do it."

"With lots of help," Anna admitted.

"I'm not sure I even want kids."

"Maybe you'll meet the guy for you and change

your mind. Maybe not. You're a kickass author, so if that's your calling in life, so be it."

"Geez, when did you get so philosophical?" Ashleigh asked with a laugh.

"Who knows? Maybe motherhood brings it out in me. Speaking of which, I'm almost home and need to get the baby down for a nap. I've got a bunch of calls to make before Jett gets home later. I've got everything booked for the wedding and reception but just need to firm up a few details."

"It's so close! I can't believe you'll be a married woman soon. Shoot. We didn't even have a bridal shower or anything like that. Should I plan a bachelorette party? It'll be last minute—not unlike the wedding—but Jen and I could take you out. We'll see who else is available."

Anna laughed. "I don't think I even have time for a bachelorette party. I've got actual Christmas presents to buy and wrap, some baking to do…. Who am I kidding? I don't bake. Lena promised to bake Christmas cookies for us. Maybe when Brody is older, I'll learn."

"Sounds like a plan. We do need to figure out a time for me to get the dress to you. I can bring it to you but need to make sure Jett's not around, because a white wedding gown isn't suspicious or anything."

"Yeah, I don't think even I could talk my way out of that," Anna admitted. "I'll text you later, okay? I'm pulling up to the gate at our home."

"Sounds good. Talk to you soon!"

Anna pushed the button to end the call and then pulled up to the gate, the receiver in her car allowing it to open automatically. All the men at Shadow Security had the code to get in, but Jett had sensors in their cars so she didn't even need to roll down her window. She smiled as the big gate swung open and she pulled into their driveway.

"Home sweet home, Brody!" she said, pulling up the long driveway. Jett's large home stood in the distance, an imposing structure. The garage door opened, and she let out a squeal of excitement. In two weeks' time, she and Jett would finally be man and wife.

Chapter 8

Jett muttered a curse as he hurried toward the office on Sunday afternoon. West had some pressing information for him regarding the Susco case. Peter Susco wasn't supposed to be working over the weekend but had shown up on the video feed. West had put a keyboard tracer on Susco's workstation, and when they realized he was unexpectedly in the office on a Sunday, began monitoring him.

Jett was concerned over the newest developments. Although his men had only been onsite for a week, he'd hoped to have handed this over to the Feds by now. The case wasn't as cut and dry as he'd hoped, with Peter Susco being the only player. Someone else was involved.

He swiped his badge at the door and moved inside Shadow Security Headquarters, eyeing the empty receptionist desk. Clara was off for the weekend, and Jett's gaze tracked to the Christmas tree and mistletoe.

He shook his head. Anna got a kick out of decorating, and the rest of the staff seemed to appreciate the holiday cheer. He still needed to get her a Christmas present. Anna had been distracted over the weekend. Giddy, almost. He knew she'd been excited about her big surprise, but she seemed even more fired up than usual. He planned to get her some sexy red lingerie, since she enjoyed the finer things in life, but he needed a bigger gift. Lena had already booked a trip for them. His assistant had smiled indulgently at his request, and Jett had realized she knew what was going on as well.

He needed to plan a surprise for Anna. Everyone seemed to know her big secret, and the trip wasn't exactly a surprise either. Maybe he should book her a spa day or schedule family photos. She did adore the one's they'd taken when Brody was a newborn, but he was already several months old and had changed so much.

Pushing thoughts of Christmas to the back of his mind, Jett moved down the secure hallway, flipping on the lights to his office. Gray and Sam were on their way, planning to review the newest information with him. He logged into his computer and frowned at the emails West had sent him, scanning over the screenshots. It appeared that Susco had been working with someone on the IT staff—which would damn well explain why he hadn't been caught by them.

"Motherfucker," he spat out.

"What's up, boss?" Gray asked, striding in.

Jett nodded to an empty chair. "Susco's been working with someone on the inside. He's hidden his tracks so well because he's got someone in IT working with him. They helped to cover it up."

Gray muttered a curse. "That would damn well explain why the Feds couldn't narrow down who was behind the leak," Gray said, scrubbing a hand over his jaw. "Susco was hiding his tracks extremely well for someone not in IT."

"Affirmative. DOD was so busy analyzing everyone in Susco's branch as they attempted to find the mole that someone in IT was about to get away scot-free."

"Unless Susco eventually ratted them out," Gray said. "He hasn't been arrested yet, right? He might be willing to talk for a price."

Jett nodded, thoughtful. "That's a possibility," he agreed. "West already hacked into the emails though. We've got proof of at least one person's involvement. It's up to DOD to decide when they want to bring them in."

Gray shook his head. "I still don't get why he's being so obvious on the surveillance footage."

"He might not know where the cameras are outside. And as for inside his office? He's got no idea West has eyes on him. We can't see inside the SCIF, but West has the electronic communications. We've got emails and timestamps for when he accessed the secure databases."

Sam came hurrying in the open office door, grabbing the other empty seat. "Sorry it took me so long to get here. The massive intelligence leak was just on the news," he said, his face filled with anger. "The latest information Susco shared gave the classified locations of our personnel in the Middle East. It's available on the dark web for anyone to find."

Jett clenched his fists, anger rising within him.

Betraying the U.S. with information on known terror cells was bad enough, but leaking the locations of those in the intelligence community? Sharing where U.S. military troops were heading? Heads needed to roll.

"God damn," Gray muttered. "The media was bound to pick up on the story before long, but hell. Susco and whoever he's working with will be more careful now. The reporters might've ruined the rest of the investigation."

"It sure the hell won't make our job easier. We have enough on Susco and one of the IT staff for the Feds to make an arrest, but DOD wanted to know everyone involved. Arresting them would show our hand. This latest breach puts multiple lives in danger," Jett fumed. "If the Feds weren't anxious to arrest him before, the news story might change everything. I'll put a call in to my contact when we're through here. As far as I'm concerned, we're still onsite in Boston until we finish our job or they call us off. Either way, Peter Susco's days as a free man are numbered."

"What do you need us to do?" Sam asked.

"West asked for someone else to be at the building in Boston. The staff knows he and Nick arrived together. He doesn't want the IT staff to grow suspicious with Nick asking questions. I need someone else to go in, but you'll have to pretend you don't know either of them. We'll need an entirely new cover story. West gained access to the emails, but DOD was adamant we be certain that only one person in IT is involved. Let's cover all our bases."

"Understood, boss. We'll handle it."

"In the meantime, I'm going to have the staff here

send some fake cables to the Boston office. It'll look like new, raw intelligence. West is going to limit who receives each cable. If anything in the fake cables is released, we'll know who is to blame."

"Hell," Gray said, looking impressed. "That's devious but just might work."

"Everyone will be on high alert now that the mainstream media has the story. We don't have any time to waste. We've got another traitor to find."

"Jesus," Sam said, rolling his shoulders. "And here I was hoping things would slow down before the holidays."

Gray smirked and glanced at his teammate. "No such luck." His eyes shifted to Jett. "How about you, boss? Any big holiday plans?"

Sam elbowed Gray, and Jett muttered another curse. "Even you two know about this? Anna's big secret?"

"Pretty sure everyone knows about her surprise but you, boss," Sam said with a grin.

Jett shook his head. "I'd demand that you tell me if she wasn't so excited about it. Enough about my fiancée and Christmas. Let's write some fake cables. West will filter who gets each one at the Boston DOD office, and then it's go time. We'll wait and see what intelligence is leaked and get our mole."

Chapter 9

Jett strode into his silent home on Friday night, taking in the quiet. He'd texted Anna to let her know he'd be staying late at the office. Again. Although he preferred spending his evenings with her, the situation couldn't be helped. He'd pulled Nick from Boston this week, sending him along with Sam, Gray, Luke, and Ford to Sudan. That meant he'd had to fill in on the Boston op for a day. It was simple work, gathering intel by chatting up the people there and getting a feel for the situation. Jett hadn't been able to stay in Boston since he needed to be at headquarters to monitor the situation overseas.

There'd been no additional leaks of classified information since the media blasted the news everywhere last weekend. None of the IT staff had taken the bait with the fake cables the Shadow Ops Team had sent. They were at a standstill. Jett turned over screenshots of the emails between Susco and the

IT staff to the Defense Department, but they hadn't ruled out the involvement of anyone else. Yet.

He rubbed his temples, his head throbbing. He'd been toying with the idea of hiring additional men, and it might be damn well time—after the new year, that is. Christmas was just over a week away. Anna had been busy wrapping presents and preparing everything, saying they needed to be ready for both Brody's first Christmas and their tropical escape afterwards. She'd pulled out suitcases and bikinis and seemed to have purchased a random assortment of other things, with various packages arriving. She'd tucked most of it away into a spare closet, telling him not to worry about it.

Ha. Luckily, he wasn't interested in snooping.

They'd have next weekend at home and then Christmas, with their getaway a few days later. Lena was a godsend and had taken care of everything regarding their travel plans. The nanny was set to stay at their home and watch Brody for several days, and he and Anna would be sitting in first class on a flight to a tropical paradise.

His gut churned at the idea of leaving his son, but he had cameras everywhere, monitoring his house and property. The team had offered to keep an eye on his home as well. He was a little surprised they'd encouraged the vacation, but he rarely took a personal day. Anna was more excited than ever, promising he'd get his big surprise before their vacation.

Jett pushed up his sleeves, revealing his muscled forearms, and moved into the quiet kitchen. The dishes were put away, and the lights from the Christmas tree out back shone brightly. He crossed over to flip off the switch and close the blinds, noticing that Anna had left him a note on the table.

Dinner's in the fridge. Just heat it up a few minutes. xoxo

Something stirred in his chest. Leave it to her to take care of him even when she was no doubt exhausted. She'd been working more than the part-time hours they'd agreed upon after she'd returned from maternity leave, and guilt coursed through him. Although Jett had been the one to insist she not come back full time yet, he needed the help. He scrubbed a hand over the scruff on his jaw, deciding he wasn't really hungry. He'd gotten a decent lunch and had made due with a protein bar earlier. He was tired, the strain from the past week catching up to him, and wanted nothing more than to crawl into bed beside Anna.

Moving down the hallway, he stuck his laptop bag in his office. He'd have to be up bright and early to touch base with his team, but they could reach him by phone if needed during the night. He might not be at Uncle Sam's beck and call anymore, but when his men were on a mission, he was always on duty. The responsibility weighed on him, but Jett wouldn't have it any other way.

Quietly pushing open the bedroom door, he stilled. The dim light on the nightstand was turned on, and Anna rustled in her sleep, sensing he was there. She opened her eyes and drowsily smiled at him, looking so damn beautiful it made his chest hurt. He strode into their room, unable to stop the smile that spread across his face at seeing her. She'd been a much lighter sleeper ever since having Brody, but he still felt guilty he'd woken her up.

"Hi baby," she said, her voice heavy with sleep.

Jett crossed the room and set his phone on the nightstand, then ducked down to kiss Anna's forehead. She still smelled of peaches and cream, so damn ripe and tempting. They were both exhausted though because of the late hour, and as much as he'd enjoy making love to her, right now, they needed their rest.

His gaze drifted to the baby monitor on the nightstand, which was alongside a stack of presents.

"What are those presents for?" he asked, his lips quirking.

"Presents for the gift exchange at the office."

"We don't have a gift exchange," Jett said with a frown.

"We do now."

He chuckled despite himself, his head already feeling better now that he was home, about to crawl into bed beside Anna. He'd get a kick out of seeing the Shadow Ops Team exchange presents, but no doubt Anna would easily talk them all into it.

"Go back to sleep," he said in a low voice. "You must be exhausted."

"That was going to be my line," she said sweetly. "Was your work stuff okay?"

"Hush," he said, turning off the lamp. He ran his hand briefly down her hair in the dark, soothing her. His thumb skimmed over her plush lips, and he kissed her briefly. "I'll tell you more about it tomorrow."

"Okay," she said, unsuccessfully trying to stifle a yawn.

Jett pulled off his polo shirt and pushed down his pants, stepping out of both them and his shoes. He undid the clasp on his watch, listening to the heavy thud as he dropped it on the nightstand, then fell into bed beside his fiancée.

"Hold me," she said, snuggling up against him.

His arms immediately wrapped around her, pulling her close. Anna's head rested on his chest, her breasts pressing against him, and her bare legs twined with his. She seemed to be wearing a silky nightie, but he wasn't about to start stripping her bare now. It was late, and they had no idea what time Brody would wake up. "Go back to sleep," he said, his lips brushing against her temple. "We'll talk in the morning."

"Okay," she whispered, her body relaxing against him. "I sleep better when you're here."

"I know."

He felt her huff of amusement before she yawned again, nestling even closer. Jett ran his hand over her silky hair and began to drift off himself, exhausted yet content in the knowledge that he was home, his family safe and secure.

Chapter 10

Two days later, Anna smiled as she twirled in front of the mirror in her wedding gown. Ashleigh gasped from across the room, tears filling her eyes. "Oh my gosh. You look incredible. Amazing. I can't believe you're really getting married this week—five short days away." Ashleigh quickly glanced to the window, as if Jett would magically appear home at that instant.

"Oh, he's not here," Anna said with a wave of her hand. "He's swamped at work with two different ops. I think some of the guys are coming home today— not that I'm supposed to know anything about it. He'll be busy for a while, which gives me all the time in the world to try on my wedding gown."

"Knock, knock!" Lena said, knocking on the open bedroom door. "I'm heading out. Wow. You look simply breathtaking."

Anna beamed, smiling at the other woman.

"I think I've got everything set for Friday—as

much as we can hide at the house, at any rate. The cases of wine and champagne are stacked in the storage closet. The place cards and table numbers are printed. The caterer is handling linens, place settings, etc. As soon as Jett leaves for the office on Friday, they'll be coming in to start setting up. The florist and bakery will deliver everything in the morning. The caterers and bartender will arrive in the afternoon."

"What about the tent?" Anna asked.

"That's scheduled as well. It'd be unlikely for Jett to come home early, but it will be just a few days before Christmas. The team knows to keep him in the office. If not, I'll keep him away from the house."

"This is getting real," Ashleigh said with a laugh. "I'll be there helping Lena run things to make sure it all goes smoothly."

"I can't wait to see his face. Jett's not really an emotional guy—more gruff and alpha, if you know what I mean. What?" Anna asked, looking at Ashleigh and Lena's amused expressions.

"We know," Ashleigh said with a laugh.

"Right. Well, nothing fazes him. I can't wait to see the look on his face. He'll be floored."

"He'll be married," Lena said with a smile.

"That too," Anna said, pointing a finger at Lena. She smoothed her hands over her still flat stomach and then twirled around in a circle, looking at herself in the full-length mirror.

"How's Jett at dancing?" Ashleigh asked.

"We never really dance, actually. I've got a great playlist though. Fortunately, Lena hooked me up with a DJ, because that was another thing I forgot. Thank goodness you're so organized," she said, flashing the woman a grateful smile.

"I've worked for Jett for many years but have honestly never seen him so happy as when he's with you."

"You're too sweet," Anna said.

"I'd say it must be true," Ashleigh agreed. "He's kind of gruff and growly but was protective of you from that very first night. Remember when you called us from the car?"

"How could I forget?" Anna asked with a giggle. She let out a contented sigh. "All right, I guess I should get out of this wedding dress and tuck it away in the back of the closet before Jett comes home. My wedding night lingerie is hidden in there, too."

"Where are you staying that night?" Ashleigh asked.

"A ritzy hotel in Manhattan. I've never spent a night away from Brody yet, and now I'll be gone several nights within the same week."

"I'm sure Jett will keep you distracted," Ashleigh teased.

Anna waggled her eyebrows. "Please. I'll be distracting him."

"And that's my cue to leave," Lena said. "I'll text you later if I've got any new updates. Otherwise, I'll see you later this week."

Lena hurried back out of the doorway to finish running errands, and Anna shot her best friend a grin. "This is really happening, girlfriend. In five days, I'll be a married woman."

Chapter 11

Jett sat at his laptop in the kitchen that evening, reviewing the latest updates. While the men who'd been in Sudan were back stateside, and he'd spent the day briefing with them at headquarters, he still had the Boston case pressing on his mind. Jett clicked on the information West had forwarded, frowning. He scanned over the email, but before he could fully review it, his phone began buzzing.

"West," he said as he lifted the phone to his ear.

"Did you see what I just sent over, boss?" West asked. Jett could hear others talking in the background, the staff at Shadow Security still hard at work trying to wrap up the case. After two weeks in Boston, West had returned to New York two days ago, working things from headquarters. He was as irritated as Jett at the traitors working at DOD and wanted to determine all the dirty players involved.

"Affirmative. Some of the information leaked,"

Jett said. "I'm just reading over your update now."

"The IT staff in Boston sat on the fake cables we sent for an entire week. I programmed a bot to scour the dark web for them. We all knew the DOD employees would be more careful after the media story but I had a feeling they'd be unable to sit on the fake intelligence for long."

"Money talks," Jett pointed out.

"That it does. Someone purchased the false information from the mole in the IT department and posted it online."

"You got a name?" Jett asked.

"Caroline Hayes. She's a Fed, not a contractor like Susco. History of discipline problems in the office but still maintains a clearance."

"Not for long. I'll get my contact at DOD on the phone. They've been itching to make an arrest. If we've got the names to hand over, they'll be ready to move."

"They can get Peter Susco and Rob McIntyre, the man he was emailing on the IT staff who helped to cover Susco's tracks, but Caroline Hayes is in the wind."

"Motherfucker," Jett bit out, clenching a fist. "You're kidding me. We finally get a name, and she's gone?"

"She didn't show up to work the past few days. She didn't call out sick or have prearranged leave either. She just didn't come to the office. They even sent security to her home to check on her. She was disliked because of her attitude, but there wasn't anything that made me suspect she was involved in the intelligence leaks until the fake cable she alone received was posted online."

"You think she took the money and bailed?"

"Maybe so. Or she grew suspicious of my being there. Either way, she's gone."

"Caroline Hayes," he muttered, anger seeping through him. "I'll google her name after I let DOD know. With three people involved, they'll be wanting to make arrests. Good work, West."

"Thanks, boss. I'll let you know if I discover anything else."

Jett set his phone down as West ended the call, his gaze shifting to the doorway. Anna was leaning against the frame, looking thoughtful. "Who's this Caroline Hayes person and what has she done to piss you off?"

Jett inhaled, releasing a slow breath. "A Federal employee who's been leaking classified information. She's missing at the moment, so the Feds will have their work cut out for them trying to locate her. Then she'll be brought under arrest."

"Do you need me to track her down?" Anna quipped, smiling as she moved closer. His eyes landed on the sway of her hips in the tight jeans she had on. The denim clung to her thighs, hugging all her gorgeous curves. "I was quite adept at finding the bad guys in Seattle," she teased, referring to an ill-fated weekend shortly after she and Jett had first gotten together. Anna had ended up getting kidnapped, and he'd been beside himself trying to find her.

"I don't need you to do anything but stay safe," he said, letting his hands grip her hips as he pulled her closer. "I've got to make a call and get this taken care of. West just gave me an update, but I've got to alert my government contact."

She leaned down and brushed a quick kiss on his

forehead, and Jett noticed that Anna's eyes twinkled with mischief as she stood back up. "All right. Make your phone call. You're almost done, right?"

He nodded, wondering what she was up to.

"I'll be back in a little while. I just remembered something that I need to do."

He raised his eyebrows but watched as Anna blew him a kiss and then disappeared through the door of the kitchen. Jett longed to go after her. Brody was down for the night, and Jett had already spent most of Sunday working. Duty called, however, and he wanted to wrap up their part of this operation before Christmas. Fortunately, West had gotten him the intelligence they needed. He grabbed his cell phone, thumbing through the numbers, then swiped the screen for his contact at DOD.

***

"What are you doing, baby?" Anna asked half an hour later as she sashayed into the kitchen, her heels clicking on the floor. The satin of her skimpy negligee brushed against the top of her bare thighs, and her nipples pebbled against the lacy bodice, arousal coursing through her. Jett was seated at the table barefoot, in jeans and a polo shirt that hugged his chiseled muscles. He was all buff and brawn, masculine in a way that appealed to all of her senses. His pine scent mixed with a hint of spice filled the air, and her stomach fluttered.

Jett glanced up from his laptop and muttered a curse, his hot gaze raking over Anna in her sexy lingerie and stilettos. "Anna. You are a temptress. Are you trying to distract me into forgetting about my work?" he asked, his deep voice doing something funny to her insides.

She giggled, slowly walking toward him, a coy smile playing about her lips. "Maybe. Is it working?"

"Is it working?" he muttered. "I'm not going to be able to think about a damn thing but you all night, which poses a problem for the work I'm not going to get done." His large hands gripped the backs of her thighs as she stopped in front of him, pulling her even closer, and then he was sliding his hands up, teasing the sensitive flesh just beneath the curve of her bottom as she squirmed. "Is this what you wanted, love?"

"Um-hmm," she said, biting her lip as his hands slid higher.

Jett's hands cupped her bare ass, exposed in her thong. "I like your hands on me," she said breathily.

"I know." Without warning, he lifted Anna onto his lap as she clung to his broad shoulders, trying to steady herself. Jett was already hard as he settled her against him, his arousal prominent through his jeans. Her heels fell with a thump to the floor as her legs dangled on either side of him. "Those are sexy shoes," he observed, his eyes tracking back to her. "Maybe later you can wear them and nothing else."

"You'd like that, wouldn't you, baby?" Anna murmured.

One of Jett's hands landed on the back of her head, the other still gripping her ass, squeezing possessively. His lips were on hers in an instant, hot and demanding. She whimpered and opened to him, enjoying the taste of whiskey and man as his tongue slid into her mouth. Jett took what he wanted, angling her head just so. Anna's long hair trailed down her back, and Jett's fingers tangled in it. His cock was swelling even more beneath her, and she bucked lightly against him, demanding more.

"You're trying to tempt me, baby girl," he said as they came up for air, both of them breathing heavily. He trailed a string of scorching kisses down her slender neck, and Anna arched into him, her pussy throbbing at the feel of Jett's erection beneath her. The stubble on his jaw rubbed against her skin, the sensation causing her skin to tingle. He was rough and raw, self-assured and taking what he wanted. She might've come to him just now, but Jett was the one in complete control.

"Tempt you? Maybe," she said, gasping as her head fell back. He palmed the back of her head gently but then nipped at her neck, playfully swatting her ass as she giggled. "The truth, Anna."

Her arms snaked around his neck, and his gaze briefly dropped to her cleavage as the movement pushed her breasts higher. "You needed a distraction," she said sweetly, staring into those piercing eyes. "You're working late every night. The team's back. You need to come to bed with me instead of working so hard."

"I'm about to work you," he muttered, suddenly standing with her in his arms. Anna squealed in surprise, her arms and legs tightening around him, but he held her easily, carrying her down the hallway toward their bedroom. "And I'm already quite hard," he quipped.

They passed the living room, the tree glowing brightly. "Are your family's flights booked for the weekend?" he asked casually, like she wasn't squirming in his arms, her pussy rubbing against his erection with each step.

"Of course. My parents are all set to come for Christmas."

"I can't wait to meet them," he said dryly.

"They can't wait to meet you. I think you'll be in for a surprise."

Jett raised his eyebrow, and she giggled again, feeling giddy. Flights had been booked all right, but her family was coming earlier than he knew, to be there in time for the wedding.

"You're always full of surprises, sweetness," he said, his voice low and husky.

Jett lowered Anna onto the bed, coming down atop her, a wicked grin on his face. Muscled arms caged her in, and she felt the weight and heat of him pressing into her. "What should I do now that I have you pinned beneath me, sweet Anna?"

"I'm sure you'll think of something," she declared.

He chuckled darkly, ducking down for more achingly sweet kisses. She was lost in him, helpless to his strength and touch. Jett ground into her, knowing exactly what he was doing. Her legs were spread wide, the denim of his jeans rubbing against her bare thighs, but it was his thick length that was driving her crazy. "I can think of lots of things," he said, his voice deep with desire. "Most of them involve fewer clothes."

"Most?"

"Mmm-hmm," he murmured, lowering his head once more and nipping at her neck. Anna shivered beneath him, feeling one of his hands trailing down the side of her body. Jett never could resist touching her, and she always loved the feel of his rough hands on her skin.

"You smell good," she murmured as Jett moved

over her. "All masculine and spicy."

He kissed his way across her collarbone before rubbing the stubble of his jaw against her breasts. "Mmm. So do you. Sweet and sexy, but I'm about to make sure every inch of you smells just like me instead." He nuzzled against her cleavage once more, and then Anna moaned as Jett's lips caught her nipple through the lace bodice of her lingerie. It was sexy and erotic feeling his wet tongue through the material, and she felt her panties dampen.

Jett lightly bit her nipple before laving it with his tongue, leaving her gasping for breath. Arousal shot straight to her core, and Jett smiled as he watched her breasts rising and falling, knowing the effect he always had on her.

"Jett," she pleaded as he turned his attention to her other breast, clearly in no hurry. He suckled at her once again, teasing her peaked nipple through the lace. His big hand palmed her other breast, his thumb skating over the tender bud.

"Yes?" he asked, his voice husky with desire. Another nip. Another swipe of his tongue.

"You're teasing me," she whimpered, her pussy throbbing.

"I am," he agreed, his thick fingers finally tugging the lace bodice down, baring her breasts to him. "So damn pretty," he said, his eyes heating. "You know I can't ever resist you, but why would I jump to the main course when I can feast on you all night?" He kissed his way across her cleavage, his stubble raking over her skin. His scent and strength surrounded her, and she felt consumed by him, ready to go up in flames.

"Are you wet for me?" he asked, one thumb

rubbing her nipple again before he pinched it gently. She gasped, whimpering.

"Why don't you find out," she breathed, trying to buck up against him as he chuckled.

"You're trouble, sweet Anna," he said. "Trouble wrapped in a sexy, gorgeous package, but trouble nonetheless."

"Is that why you proposed to me a year ago?"

He smiled, his gaze tracking to the diamond ring on her finger. "Among other reasons." He shifted slightly, and his hand slid up her inner thigh, squeezing it gently before caressing her pussy. "You're wearing too many clothes," he said, his fingers trailing up her seam over the smooth satin. Her thong was soaked, and she knew Jett could feel her silken arousal. He circled her clit through the material, and she moaned as he held her in place. "Mine," he murmured, his thick finger circling her swollen bud.

"I need you inside me," she pleaded.

"You need to come first," he ordered, his mouth on her breast again as he continued to toy with her clit. She gasped and cried out as his fingers moved faster, his tongue flickering over one nipple. The dual sensations were mind-blowing, and she writhed beneath him, moaning. He pushed her panties aside, and then his fingers were trailing through her silken folds, urging her toward an orgasm.

"Jett—oh God—" she panted.

"I love how slick you are. Hot. Wet. So ready for me." Two thick fingers slid into her core, and he thrust them in and out as her inner walls clamped down around him. "You're so close, sweet girl." His thumb pressed against her clit and then circled faster, never relenting. Heat coiled within her, spiraling down from her belly. Jett laved at her nipple again while thrusting his fingers into her pussy, and as he rubbed over her clit once more, she screamed out his name, shattering apart in his arms.

Jett finally pulled his fingers from her molten core and gently caressed her folds, bringing her back down from her orgasmic high. It was erotic to see his big hand at her sex, his muscled arm between her thighs. He'd always been big and strong, and she'd always been at his complete and utter mercy. He kissed one nipple and then the other, leaving her filled with a want she couldn't explain. It was sexy and exhilarating, yet somehow tender, too, his hands and lips on her most sensitive parts. Jett knew every square inch of her body and exactly how to drive her wild, and he thrilled at making her come undone.

He rolled them over so Anna was draped atop him, her breasts still spilling over the top of her negligee. His hands were everywhere, caressing and soothing.

"Your turn," she said a few minutes later, trying to move off him.

"Nuh-uh," he chastised. "I'm in charge tonight." Jett easily positioned her, putting Anna on her hands and knees. His hand skimmed over her backside, and then he tugged down her skimpy thong, baring her to his gaze. She heard him unzipping his pants, and then he was moving closer, his thick cock pressing against her. Jett reached beneath Anna, rubbing her clit as he softly kissed her neck. He surrounded her, controlling her pleasure even now

"Take me," she pleaded, reaching back to grab hold of him.

He pressed impossibly closer, his erection sliding through her folds. She wiggled against him, and then Jett was lining himself up again, notching himself at her core.

"I love you," he said, pushing all the way in with one powerful thrust. She gasped at his penetration, Jett stretching her in a way that would leave her deliciously sore tomorrow. He always felt so big taking her from behind, and Anna whimpered knowing she was at his complete mercy. His forearm held her tightly, his hand possessively palming one breast. "Shhh," he murmured, kissing the back of her neck again. She relaxed as he began to move, slowly pulling out and pushing back in, filling her completely. His thick erection stroked her inner walls, the exquisite pressure nearly too much to bear. She cried out as he shifted once more, his fingers playing with her clit.

Anna clawed at the sheets, gasping as he took his time, teasing her. His lips were on her bare skin again, the scruff of his jaw erotic and sensual. His throbbing cock stretched her pussy to accommodate his size, and his fingers on her clit were unrelenting.

"Come for me," he urged, beginning to take her faster. Harder.

"Jett," she wailed, bucking back against him as her legs began to shake.

He filled her completely, making her his in every way. He thrust into her again, and as his fingers pinched her clit, she screamed, her pussy spasming around him as waves of pleasure washed over her. Jett bucked into her twice more and came as well, groaning her name on his release. He hovered over her a moment, his forearm locked around her, his cock buried deep inside her still spasming pussy. They were both breathing hard as he finally pulled out and collected her in his arms. She felt flushed and sated, safe as he held her close. Her body draped over his, both of them covered in a fine sheen of sweat.

"I love you," he murmured, his lips caressing her temple.

"I love you too, baby," she said, smiling contentedly as his hands moved over her, warm and soothing.

"Sleep," he said as she quietly yawned. "I've got to finish up with my work but will be back soon."

"You better be," she said drowsily as he chuckled. And then she was drifting off to sleep, safe in his arms, mere days away from becoming his wife.

Chapter 12

Five days later, Anna was impatiently tapping her foot on the kitchen floor. Jett was always up and out the door early, ready to get a head start at the office. It figured that today—their surprise wedding day—he was taking his sweet time to leave. Aside from the woman who'd gone AWOL, the case Jett had been wrapped up with seemed to be nearly over. There'd even been a big news story the other day about the arrest of two Defense Department employees who'd been leaking information. Although Jett couldn't tell her the details of their classified ops, she'd gotten the gist of it thanks to all of the media coverage.

"You look impatient, sweetness," Jett said as he strode into the kitchen, brushing a kiss against her temple.

"Just a lot to do today," she said, glancing at the clock on the stove.

"Uh-huh," he said, nothing slipping by him as his gaze tracked her movements.

She lifted a shoulder. "Christmas is only a few days away. I've got lots to do. It is our baby's first Christmas, after all."

"And then after that, we'll be jetting off on a tropical vacation," he said, his voice husky.

"Can't wait!" she said too brightly, and he raised his eyebrows. "You need to head into the office," she urged. "I've got last-minute stuff to do and need the house to myself."

"I don't suppose that's why a white van kept driving by earlier," he asked with a smirk.

Anna playfully swatted at him. "You're too observant sometimes. Just promise me you won't look at the security cameras today and ruin the preparations I'm making for your surprise. Please?" she pleaded.

Jett's muscular arms wrapped around her waist as he pulled her close. "You know I can't deny you anything," he said, ducking for a heated kiss. Anna was flushed when they finally came up for air. "If I didn't have to really leave for the office, I'd have you crying out my name again," he said, his eyes hot. She smiled coyly at him, recalling the way he'd pleasured her that morning, waking her up with his head buried between her thighs. She'd been writhing against his mouth as Jett ate her out, and she'd helplessly cried out his name as he'd made her come again and again.

"Let's save that thought for tonight," she said with a wink. "And if Lena tells you to do anything today, just go with it."

Jett barked out a laugh. "She works for me, not the other way around."

"Jett," Anna said sternly, trying to level him with a glare.

"All right, sweetness," he said, brushing his lips over hers in a chaste kiss. "I'll be good—for now. After this big surprise, all bets are off."

"That's all I'm asking for," she said, playfully pushing him to the door. She smiled as she watched him leave the kitchen, and a moment later, she heard the garage door opening. "Finally," she breathed, rushing over to her cell phone. She had tons of last-minute things to do and had to get ready herself. Operation Mistletoe Mischief was about to take flight.

***

Jett grumbled as he noticed his men eyeing him speculatively later that morning. Everyone seemed to be in high spirits, and it wasn't just because of the upcoming holiday weekend. Christmas was only days away, and barring any emergencies, he and his team would be off for several days next week. Essential personnel would be staffing the building, and Luke would be in charge of anything urgent that arose while Jett was on vacation. He was looking forward to escaping for a few days with Anna to some sunshine and sand, although they'd both miss their infant son.

"What?" Jett jokingly growled, watching Sam eye him with a shit-eating grin.

"Nothing, boss," Sam said. "Just happy it's Friday."

"Bullshit. All of you know what's going on, and I don't like it."

Ford chuckled from where he stood near Clara at the receptionist's desk. Someone had baked a ridiculous amount of Christmas cookies, and they were spread out across the counter on festive platters. Jett watched as Ford snagged a gingerbread man, taking a bite. "Gotta admit, these hit the spot. Plus, they saved me from doing a donut run," he joked.

Clara flushed beside him, and Ford affectionately ruffled her hair. "Of course, I don't mind running out at lunch," he assured her. "You and Anna are easy to please with something sweet. The rest of these guys are heathens," he joked.

"I notice Anna's not here today, boss," Nick said as his lips quirked. "Thought she was coming in on Fridays."

"Enough," Jett ground out. "All of you know her surprise. I get it."

Sam crossed his arms, laughing quietly. "It kills you to not know what's going on—just admit it."

"I'll do no such thing."

Bells jingled on the front door, and then Anna herself breezed into the lobby. Her hair was freshly done, with long, blonde waves cascading down her back. Her cheeks were flushed, and her blue eyes sparkled with amusement. Jett raised his eyebrows. "I've decided we're celebrating tonight," Anna declared. "Lena's bringing something for you to wear—either a suit or a tux," she added, almost as an afterthought. "We'll get all dressed up and go out."

"And what are we celebrating?" Jett asked dryly. "Please promise me we're not sitting through an opera or something."

Anna shot him a look of disbelief as the rest of the guys howled with laughter. Gray cleared his throat, still chuckling. "It's definitely not an opera."

"Please, even I can't sit through those," Anna said. She wrapped her arms around Jett's neck as she rose on her tiptoes for a kiss. He indulged her, and then she ran her hands down the front of his chest. "Don't be so grumpy," she said.

"I'm not grumpy. I just don't like not knowing what's going on."

"You'll know everything tonight," she said, smiling reassuringly. "I'll be at home getting ready this afternoon because I want to 'wow' you, so you need to stay at the office until dinner."

"Anna—"

"No ifs, ands, or buts about it. You always work late, so I'm sure it's no big deal for a control freak like you to make sure everything is running smoothly today," she teased. "But you have to come home at exactly six-thirty. Don't show up earlier, because I'll be so mad at you. Promise me that you won't ruin the surprise."

"Don't worry, it's a good one, boss," Luke said.

The doors to the basement opened just then, and West strode into the lobby, frowning. "What's wrong?" Jett asked.

"I just got word that Caroline Hayes might be in Manhattan. Her sister lives there. It turns out that she might not be completely missing after all."

"Where in Manhattan?" Anna asked. Jett shot her a look. "I know. I'll stay out of it. Promise," she assured him.

West cleared his throat. "The Feds are working with the NYPD. They're planning to move in and make an arrest later this afternoon."

"That's the best news I've heard all day," Jett said.

Anna giggled as the others exchanged looks. "Just wait, baby. You might change your mind later on after you find out my surprise. I've got to get a few more things done before tonight, so I've got to head out. Remember. Six-thirty."

"Six-thirty," Jett repeated. "And I'll wear whatever Lena has for me."

"Thanks, baby!" Anna said, giving him another quick kiss. She said goodbye to the others and then hurried back across the lobby. She waved from the doorway, waggling her fingers. "I'll see you tonight. Don't work too hard," she said with a wink. "And good luck finding that Caroline chick."

Jett raised his eyebrows.

She blew him a kiss before turning to leave.

He shook his head, looking back at his men. "This better be some surprise," he said.

"I promise that you'll love it," Clara told him quietly.

He nodded at her in thanks and relaxed slightly. While his men would get a kick out of whatever Anna had planned, he knew Clara would be honest with him. "Let's get back to work then. I've got to finalize some things before my trip next week. West, keep me updated on the situation involving Caroline Hayes."

"Will do," West replied. "We'll wrap this case up with a nice little bow."

"Or a knot," Sam joked. "Like how you tie a knot?" Nick elbowed him as the others tried to keep straight faces. Looking around at everyone assembled in the lobby again, Jett turned and headed toward his office, shaking his head. He was itching to know what Anna was up to, but it sounded like tonight he'd finally have his answers.

Chapter 13

"A tux?" Jett asked Lena later that afternoon, eyeing the black tuxedo she'd brought him. A pair of black dress shoes in a box were sitting on his desk, no doubt Anna's doing.

"She's very excited about tonight," Lena said casually, sliding her cell phone back into her purse. "Go get dressed, and I'll see you later on. I've got a few details to help Anna with. We've got to make sure the big surprise goes off without a hitch."

Jett leveled her with a look.

"Be nice," she chastised.

"No hints?" he asked, taking the boutonniere she handed him. Lena had kept his life organized for years, but normally he was the one giving directions.

"No hints," she said. "Clara said she could help pin that on if you have any trouble. She'll be here her regular hours today. Anna's already back at home.

Don't be late tonight," she added before saying goodbye and heading out the door.

He shook his head, his lips quirking as she left. His Anna was something else. He imagined they were going into Manhattan for the evening to some special event. He didn't hate the idea of seeing Anna in a gorgeous dress and sexy heels. He'd noticed earlier that she'd gotten her hair done, her long, blonde strands falling in lush waves down her back. He loved her hair like that, especially after he undressed her. There was something about the way it teased her bare breasts that drove him absolutely wild.

He picked up his phone to call Anna and was surprised when Ashleigh answered it for her. There sounded like a lot of commotion in the background, and he frowned.

"Oh, hi Jett!" Ashleigh said. "Anna and I are running some errands. What's up?"

The noise in the background suddenly dissipated, and he tried to place the sounds. There were people talking and dishes clattering. Maybe they were at a restaurant? "I was just wondering if my better half was getting ready for her big surprise tonight."

"Oh, she is," Ashleigh assured him. "Can I pass on a message? Anna can't come to the phone at the moment."

"No thank you," he said smoothly. "I'll see her tonight. If I don't talk with you beforehand, Merry Christmas," he added.

"Merry Christmas!" she replied before ending the call.

Jett set his phone down on the desk and scrolled through the emails on his computer screen, his gaze landing on the clock. Sixteen hundred. He still had a couple of hours before he needed to leave. His mind was completely preoccupied though, with thoughts of tonight, Christmas, and their vacation next week filling his head.

His phone buzzed with a text, and he smiled as he saw West's message.

Caroline Hayes was found. NYPD arrested her ten minutes ago.

"About damn time," he said to himself, relief coursing through him. It was nice to wrap up that case before taking some time off for the holidays. His team had already done their part, but having the suspects arrested solidified a job well done. His gut churned at the knowledge that several Federal employees had been leaking classified intelligence, but they'd been brought in and would now be spending years in jail for their treachery.

He thumbed a response to West and then decided to start getting ready for the evening. After showering in the locker room downstairs, he returned to his office. Jett took his time putting on his tuxedo, imagining Anna dressing as well. She always seemed to have sexy bra and panty sets, and he wondered what lingerie she'd be wearing tonight. She looked beautiful in everything she wore, but he appreciated the effort she always took to look nice.

He fastened his cufflinks, rotating his wrist as he finished adjusting them. Eyeing the boutonniere that Lena had dropped off, he carefully pinned it to his lapel. It was deep red, and briefly, he wondered if he should've gotten Anna flowers. It was difficult to know what to bring home when he didn't even know what they were doing this evening. Then again, Lena would've arranged for whatever he needed.

The office was quiet as he finally walked through the lobby, the Christmas tree still twinkling. That empty lobby was somewhat unusual, but it was the last day of work before the long weekend and Christmas. He'd stayed later than most people. No doubt many of the team would be eager to get home to their wives or girlfriends for some family time. Taking one last look around, he exited through the front door. Tonight felt important, somehow. He couldn't quite put a finger on it, but everyone had been excited for him—for Anna's big surprise. She'd already announced her pregnancy, so it wasn't that. They already had a trip planned next week.

Jett realized he was excited. It was just like Anna to put in all this effort to surprise him. She loved to go all out and was a wildcard sometimes, but he loved that about her.

Twenty minutes later, Jett was turning onto his street. Briefly, he registered all the cars at his neighbor's house as he drove along the secluded road. The houses were spread out, each on large lots of land with wooded property in the back. He appreciated the privacy and briefly wondered what sort of celebration his neighbors were having as he passed by. It was hard to see in the dark, but he noticed some catering vans out front. It looked like quite the event.

The gate to his own property opened, and he pulled up the long driveway. The house looked normal, the Christmas tree in the living room displayed in the front window. The blinds were shut on the other windows, but it was dark out. He preferred for passersby not to see inside his home at night. As he climbed out of his car and shut the door, he could almost sense the excitement in the air. Something was going on, he realized as his garage door closed.

"Anna!" he called out as he walked inside.

The house was quiet without her moving around—eerily quiet. Jett didn't like it. He moved down the hall to the kitchen, expecting to see some of her belongings scattered about. A purse. A coat. Those sexy heels she wore that drove him wild. The back blinds to the deck were closed, but with a cursory glance around the kitchen, he could tell she hadn't been in here recently.

He moved to the bedroom, seeing that it was also empty, and then he headed to his son's nursery. The room was dark and silent. Uneasiness washed over him. Anna had been adamant that he arrive home at this exact time. Even Lena had mentioned that he shouldn't be late. Certainly, the nanny would be here to watch Brody if Jett and Anna were going out for the night. He tried calling Anna's cell phone and then cursed as he heard it ringing in their bedroom down the hall.

"Anna!" he called out loudly, suddenly growing alarmed. She definitely wouldn't have left without her phone. Jett swiped the screen on his phone as he moved into their bedroom, realizing her purse was on the nightstand. He scrolled his contact list and called Luke.

"Anna's missing," he barked out. "I just got home, and the house is quiet. She left her phone and purse in the bedroom. Her car's in the garage. Something's wrong."

"Boss, she's not missing," Luke assured him. Jett could almost hear the amusement in his voice. "Take a deep breath and come out on your back deck."

"What?" he asked, stilling.

Luke cleared his throat. "Come out on the back deck," he repeated. "I'm pretty sure Anna is ready."

"You're kidding me," Jett muttered, strolling back through his home. He moved down the hallway toward the kitchen again. "Anna's in the backyard?"

"See you soon," Luke quipped before hanging up.

Jett stared at his phone for a beat, dumbfounded. Luke was out there, too? He shoved his phone into his pocket, scrubbing a hand over his jaw. Worry competed with anticipation. She was okay, and whatever this surprise was, he'd find out in mere moments. Not bothering to open the blinds, Jett pulled open the back door. As soon as he stepped onto the deck, the backyard was suddenly lit up with thousands of little twinkling lights. His jaw dropped in surprise as he saw a big white tent in the distance. There were chairs lined up on the grass, filled with guests. As he hustled across the deck and walked down the steps, his teammates, who'd been standing in single line, moved to the side.

Anna was standing there at the end of the aisle, dressed in a white wedding gown. Jett's jaw dropped, and he froze, taking in the moment. She was beautiful. The white satin and lace clung to her curves, and she had some type of warm wrap around her bare arms. Her long, blonde waves fell around her face, brushing against her cleavage, and it took him another second to see she was holding a bouquet of deep red flowers that matched the boutonniere he wore.

Jett moved closer, almost in a daze. He'd brought Anna out here the weekend they'd met, making love to her in his backyard under the warm autumn sun. In the cool winter air, dressed in white under the dark sky, she was breathtaking.

"Surprise," Anna said, smiling, and then Jett was hurrying toward her, rushing down the aisle. He could hear murmurs and chuckles from the crowd, but he ignored everything else, honing in on her.

"Anna, I thought something happened to you," he said, astonished. "I thought you ran off and pulled some other crazy stunt."

"Crazier than pulling off our own wedding?" she asked with a smile.

He took both of her hands, staring into her eyes. "This is the last thing I expected. I couldn't find you when I got home but knew you wouldn't leave your phone or purse. I thought you were hurt."

"Is this okay?" she asked, suddenly looking worried. Anna was a confident, bold woman, but he saw the brief flash of hesitation in her eyes.

"More than okay," he assured her. "I'm just glad you're okay. But this?" he asked, smiling down at her. "I've wanted to marry you since the moment I proposed—maybe since the night we met, when I drove you back to my house. I love you," he said, his voice thick with emotion. His thumb trailed over her knuckles, and he knew he always wanted this woman in his life. Forever. His gaze briefly tracked around the crowded backyard, and he was stunned to see his brother Slate and some of his old Army buddies there. The nanny had baby Brody all bundled up, sleeping soundly in her arms. Anna pointed out her parents, and he felt his chest filling with an emotion he couldn't express. Jett wasn't a soft man, but he felt a bit misty at the moment. This was everything.

His gaze tracked to the right, and he saw that the entire Shadow Ops Team was there. Anna's friends were seated across the aisle, and they smiled and waved. His gaze scanned over other neighbors and friends, and he shook his head in wonder.

"Shall we get married then?" Anna asked, squeezing his hands tightly.

His eyes swept back to her. "Yes. I don't want to wait another second to make you my wife."

The brief ceremony flew by in the blink of an eye, and as the officiant pronounced them man and wife, Jett pulled his new bride into his arms and kissed her deeply. The crowd began to whoop and holler, and he finally released her, chuckling as she gave him one last kiss, her red nails raking through his shortly cropped hair.

"To Jett and Anna!" one of the men shouted.

"Way to go, boss!" Sam yelled.

Everyone was standing and clapping as music began to play from the speakers in the backyard. Jett and Anna stood there beaming for a moment as the photographer snapped some pictures, and then Anna was tugging him back down the aisle as the crowd cheered them on.

"How in the world did you pull this off?" Jett asked, amazed, as they moved toward the tent for the reception.

"I had a little help," she admitted. "But I didn't want to wait another day to be your wife."

"Married by Christmas," he murmured. "I never would've guessed it. Our tropical vacation next week will be our honeymoon."

"Exactly," she said with a wink.

"Wait—is someone watching the baby tonight?" he asked huskily, his gaze dropping to her form in the snug satin gown.

"Yep, and I booked us a suite in a ritzy Manhattan hotel. We've got a late check-out, too," she added suggestively.

Jett's hands dropped to her waist, and he pulled her close, his lips at her ear. "I've never made love to my wife before," he joked. "Just my girlfriend and fiancée."

"Umm-hmm. Exactly. You'll have to practice a lot to get it right. Think you can handle that?"

Jett let his hands roam, kissing her thoroughly before the crowd began to come over. Their friends and family were gathering around them now, and a receiving line of sorts formed as their guests began streaming into the tent, offering their congratulations. As unconventional as their relationship had been, the wedding had been flawless. He had a new bride, a son, and another baby on the way. His life had turned out exactly the way it was supposed to, and it was damn perfect.

About the Author

USA Today Bestselling Author Makenna Jameison writes sizzling romantic suspense, including the addictive Alpha SEALs series.

Makenna loves the beach, strong coffee, red wine, and traveling. She lives in Washington DC with her husband and two daughters.

Visit www.makennajameison.com to discover your next great read.

Printed in Great Britain
by Amazon